"Coach, do you think our mom's pretty?" Ryan gazed up at Nathan.

Drying his hands, he took in their wide-eyed expressions, while an avalanche of questions crashed through his mind. Yeah, he thought she was pretty, but did he dare say that to her sons?

Honesty is the best policy. "Yes, your mom is very pretty."

Andrew peered up at Nathan. "Do you like her?"

Why were they peppering him with these questions—questions he didn't want to answer? "Of course, I like your mother. She is very nice."

"I knew you would." Ryan grinned as he proceeded to wash his hands.

Was his attraction to Melanie, which he'd been trying to tamp down, that apparent, even to her children? Nathan studied the photo collages that hung on the walls in the hallway. They told of happy times. Nathan could imagine how much her husband's death must have turned Melanie's world upside down. Could he be a little part of making it right again?

Books by Merrillee Whren

Love Inspired

The Heart's Homecoming
An Unexpected Blessing
Love Walked In
The Heart's Forgiveness
Four Little Blessings
Mommy's Hometown Hero
Homecoming Blessings
*Hometown Promise
*Hometown Proposal
*Hometown Dad

*Kellerville

MERRILLEE WHREN

is the winner of the 2003 Golden Heart Award for best inspirational romance manuscript presented by Romance Writers of America. In 2004, she made her first sale to Steeple Hill. She is married to her own personal hero, her husband of thirty-plus years, and has two grown daughters. She has lived in Atlanta, Boston, Dallas and Chicago but now makes her home on one of God's most beautiful creations, an island off the east coast of Florida. When she's not writing or working for her husband's recruiting firm, she spends her free time playing tennis or walking the beach, where she does the plotting for her novels. Please visit her website at www.merrilleewhren.com.

Hometown Dad
Merrillee Whren

Steeple Hill®

Published by Steeple Hill Books™

STEEPLE HILL BOOKS

Steeple
Hill®

ISBN-13: 978-0-373-87651-8

HOMETOWN DAD

Copyright © 2011 by Merrillee Whren

www.SteepleHill.com

Printed in U.S.A.

Praise be to the God and Father of our Lord Jesus Christ, the Father of compassion and the God of all comfort, who comforts us in all our troubles, so that we can comfort those in any trouble with the comfort we ourselves have received from God. For just as the sufferings of Christ flow over into our lives, so also through Christ our comfort overflows.

—2 *Corinthians* 1:3–5

To my daughter Danielle, whose positive attitude
in dealing with her Crohn's disease
inspired this story.

I would like to thank Randy Stewart
for his input on banking procedures.
All mistakes are mine.

Chapter One

Anxiety knotted Melanie Drake's stomach as she pushed open the heavy glass door leading into the Kellerville National Bank. Her seven- and eight-year-old sons, Andrew and Ryan, raced ahead, chasing each other around the deposit counter in the middle of the floor. As she tried to corral them, their laughter and the slap of their tennis shoes on the marble floor seemed to echo off the walls of the cavernous lobby with its cherry paneling and granite columns. Their misbehavior did nothing to soothe her frazzled mind.

Melanie grabbed each of the boys by an arm and pulled them to a stop. Letting go to adjust the satchel she'd slung over her shoulder, she leaned down and looked them in the eye. She forced herself not to raise her voice. "You two, settle down. Now."

When a teller gave them a disapproving look, Melanie feared her harsh whisper hadn't been as quiet as she'd intended. Staring at her wide-eyed, the boys nodded and said nothing.

"Okay, then." She tried to put on a happy face, even though nothing was going as planned today. She guided the boys to a couple of navy leather chairs situated against a wall near the bank offices. "Sit here."

Andrew and Ryan settled on the oversized chairs, and

she handed them each a book. Ryan surveyed the book, then looked up, wrinkling his nose. "Do I have to read this? It looks boring."

"I'll read it." Andrew snatched it from Ryan's hand.

"Hey, I want that." Ryan grabbed it back.

While Melanie tried to take charge of her warring sons, a stern-faced woman approached. "May we help you?"

Melanie took a calming breath and met the woman's critical gaze. "Yes, I'm Melanie Drake and I have an appointment with Nathan Keller at three-thirty."

"Mr. Keller should be with you shortly." The woman glanced at her watch, then toward the office where Nathan Keller was clearly visible through the large window. She looked down her nose at the boys before turning her attention back to Melanie. "You're welcome to wait right here."

"Thanks." Melanie sat on one of the chairs opposite Ryan and Andrew and breathed a sigh of relief as the unsmiling woman resumed her position behind a desk at the far side of the lobby.

"Mom, he touched me." Ryan pushed Andrew's arm.

Standing, Melanie glared at her sons and pointed to the chair next to hers. "Ryan, over here."

"Okay." Ryan jumped up and obeyed her orders.

After he was seated, she hunkered down between them. "I know you guys don't want to be here, but if you can't behave while I have this meeting, I won't hesitate to make my excuses and leave. You'll both be grounded, and I won't unground you until I see improvement in your behavior. Do you understand?"

They nodded, their little faces solemn, but Melanie wasn't sure they believed her. She sat down and plucked a paperback novel from her satchel. Although she tried to read, her thoughts wandered to her children. Some of their bad behavior was the result of her lax discipline since their father had died. She was working on being a better disciplinarian, but sometimes she found the task difficult. She knew how much her little boys missed their father and hated to make them feel worse by scolding them.

A single mom, she had all of the parental responsibilities, making for extra stress in her life. People from church stepped in from time to time to help her out, but it wasn't the same as having Tim there to share the parenting duties. She tried to remember that God was with her and would see her through, but she sometimes forgot that one important truth.

Every day was another step toward learning to deal with her grief. She wasn't going to let that sadness keep her from being the best parent for her boys. Loving them and caring for them was her top priority.

She'd been putting on a brave face for her sons, but some days were really hard. She'd made a lot of progress in the past two years, maybe not as much as she would have liked. She wanted Ryan and Andrew to have a bright future, and part of that meant having this meeting with someone who knew investment strategies and could help her make the first move in getting her financial life in order. That's why she was here.

Melanie glanced toward the office where Nathan Keller talked with an older couple. Could he help her? His sandy brown hair, cut in a neat short style, gave him a business-like appearance. Did his serious demeanor mean she could trust him to give her the advice she needed?

Although she was a friend of Nathan's cousin, Juliane, and they attended the same church, Melanie didn't know him very well. His father was the bank president, and his mother taught at the local college. They were prominent people in the little town of Kellerville. According to Juliane, Nathan was being groomed to take over the bank when his father retired.

Melanie had to believe Nathan could answer her financial questions.

Her stomach churning, she looked back at Ryan and Andrew and hoped she could get through the afternoon without another outburst from them. If the boys misbehaved during the meeting, she would be mortified. Would Nathan look down his nose at her the same as the woman behind the desk had?

Melanie felt as though she'd spent most of her life dealing with people who looked down on her because of her upbringing. Her late husband's parents were people like that. Ever since she'd met them, she'd been trying to show them she deserved their respect, not their disdain. She didn't want to think about them and forced herself to concentrate on her book.

"Mrs. Drake." A deep male voice startled her. "I'm sorry to keep you waiting. It's nice to see you."

"That's okay, and it's good to see you, too." Standing, Melanie looked up into Nathan's brown eyes—brown, the color of her morning tea. They exuded warmth. Despite the kindness in them, her thoughts skittered. She hadn't realized she was so nervous, but the notion of making the wrong decision about the money she'd inherited had kept her from making any decision at all. "Thanks for meeting with me."

"The bank is here to serve you."

As he shook her hand, she tried to ignore the little prickles that raced up her arm. Melanie looked over at her sons. "These are my boys, Andrew and Ryan. I didn't intend to bring them, but my sitter cancelled at the last minute. I didn't have time to find another one."

Nathan looked over at the youngsters. Melanie watched to see his reaction. He smiled. Kindness radiated from his smile just as it had from his eyes. "Hello. Which one is Ryan?"

"Me." Ryan sprang from the chair.

Not to be outdone, Andrew pushed his way in front of Ryan. "And I'm Andrew."

Melanie wanted to scold Andrew, but she'd done enough scolding already. Besides, she was too embarrassed to correct her sons in front of this man, who was a VIP in Kellerville.

Nathan shook hands with each of the boys. "I'm glad to meet you, Andrew and Ryan."

The tension in Melanie's shoulders eased as the boys politely returned Nathan's handshake. At least they remembered some of the manners she'd taught them.

Nathan escorted them into his office and indicated that Melanie should sit in the wood-frame armchair at the side of his desk. Grabbing two armless chairs, he set them in the corner in front of a small desk containing a computer. "You guys can sit here, and if you promise not to tell anyone, I'll let you play one of my games."

"We won't tell." Ryan glanced at Andrew. "Will we?"

Shaking his head, Andrew looked at Melanie, then back at Nathan. "I won't, but what about our mom?"

Winking, Nathan grinned at her. "What about it, Mom? Will you keep our secret?"

"Sure. Your secret's safe with me." Melanie noticed for the first time how Nathan's grin made a nice-looking man twice as handsome. But this wasn't the time to let a heart-stopping grin make her realize the way his broad shoulders filled out his gray-pinstriped suit. She'd barely been aware of him when they'd met in passing at church during the last two years. Why was she noticing so much about him today?

While Nathan gave the boys instructions about the game and outfitted them each with a set of headphones, Melanie tried to collect her thoughts. Despite Nathan's affability, her mind whirled. She shouldn't be this nervous. He was trying to put her at ease, but for some reason, his smile had her thoughts scrambled. She gripped the satchel and took a shaky breath. Finally, she squared her shoulders and looked at him as he settled on the chair behind his desk.

"What can I do to help you?" He smiled again.

Her heart hammered. She didn't want him to think she was a complete dunderhead, but she felt out of her league talking about investments. Trying to remember the little speech she'd practiced, she pulled a folder from the satchel and laid it on the desk. "You know I'm a hygienist in your uncle's dental practice. Dr. Joe told me that I should see you about some financial advice."

"Yes, good ole Dr. Joe. He's always looking out for his employees." Nathan patted the folder. "What do you have here?"

"My financial papers."

"What kind of financial advice are you looking for?"

"I'm not sure."

Nathan picked up the file. "May I look through this?"

Studying Nathan's demeanor as he thumbed through her papers, she hoped she hadn't made a mistake in following Dr. Joe's advice. Her boss was like the father she'd never had, and she trusted him to steer her in the right direction. But as she watched Nathan's eyebrows knit in a little frown, she worried that she'd made the wrong decision.

Finally, Nathan looked up. Warmth still radiated from his eyes, but she detected a little curiosity, as well. "There's a lot here. Do you want me to draw up a financial plan for you?"

"What exactly does that mean?"

"I can give you ideas about where to invest your money." He glanced at Andrew and Ryan, who were thankfully quiet and busy with the video game. Looking back at her, Nathan nodded his head in the boys' direction. "I imagine you want to put some of this in a college fund for them."

"Yes." Melanie nodded. "I'm sure you're wondering why it's taken me two years to do something about this."

Nathan shook his head. "No, I imagine you've had to collect yourself after a shocking, life-changing experience. Sometimes, it's better to do nothing than to make emotional decisions that you might regret later."

Melanie placed a hand over her heart. "Oh, you do understand. I just couldn't bring myself to tackle the job. Every time I thought about it I would…"

Closing her eyes, Melanie pressed her lips together. She wouldn't fall apart now. Tim was gone. She couldn't bring him back. He would always have a place in her heart, but she had to pick up *all* of the pieces of her life and move on. That included the money from Tim's life insurance that she'd let sit in the bank and his other investments that she hadn't paid enough attention to.

She summoned her courage. *The Lord is my strength and my song; he has become my salvation.* The words from a Psalm she'd recently memorized as part of her grief recovery group flitted through her mind, giving her peace for the moment. When her husband Tim had died from an aneurysm at the young age of thirty-four, she'd started the group as a church ministry. Somehow she felt as though she should have it all together by now, rather than letting memories of Tim make her feel weepy two year later.

"Are you okay?"

At the sound of Nathan's soothing voice, Melanie opened her eyes and tried to smile. "I'm sorry. I didn't mean to let this affect me. I'm doing better, but as you see, looking at this stuff brings back all the sorrow."

"So you've been putting it off?"

"Exactly. Thank you. Thank you for recognizing the difficulty I've been having." Melanie smiled. This time it was genuine, not forced. "I'm trying to move on with my life."

Nathan nodded. "You are. Just the fact that you came to see me shows that."

"Dr. Joe has been such a help to me. He and Juliane suggested that I get your financial advice. You've made me feel better already."

"Good. I'm here to help you." Nathan closed the folder. "Do you mind if I keep this and look it over more fully? That'll give me time to formulate some recommendations for you. Then we can meet again and get a better understanding of your needs."

"Okay. When would you like to get together?"

"At your convenience."

What would another meeting with Nathan bring? Melanie couldn't forget how this initial encounter made her heart race, but that was from nervousness, wasn't it? She barely knew the man. How could there be any other reason?

"Mom, he's cheating." Andrew's voice made Melanie jump, short-circuiting her response about another meeting. Embarrassed, she hurried to the corner to negotiate the peace. She'd been doing a lot of that lately.

"I'm not cheating. He's just a sore loser." Jerking off the headphones, Ryan stared at her.

Andrew also removed his headphones. "I wouldn't lose, if he didn't cheat."

"The game is over for both of you." Melanie didn't want to turn and face Nathan. What must he think after he'd been so nice to allow them to play? She couldn't slink away, although she wished she could. Gathering her courage, she turned to Nathan. "I'm sorry about this. I'd better take them home."

"That's okay. I'll give you a call after I've had time to study this." He held up the folder.

"That would be fine. Thanks." Melanie could hardly wait to make her exit as she moved toward the door.

Nathan accompanied her and opened it for her. "I'll call you in a few days."

"I'll be waiting to hear from you." As Melanie ushered her sons out of Nathan's office, she couldn't imagine what he must be thinking. It all had to be awful—everything from her sons' misbehavior to her inability to keep her emotions in check had shown her in a bad light. He must surely think she was a basket case with a couple of brats on her hands. How was she going to face him again? Maybe they could work out the details of her investments by phone and email, and she wouldn't have to see him again. But whatever happened, she wasn't going to let the investments fall by the wayside again, no matter *what* she had to do.

She'd overcome a terrible childhood, and she would make sure her kids never had to suffer the way she had.

Standing in his office door, Nathan watched Melanie and her sons leave the bank. Her dark brown hair shone in the warm sunshine of a late May afternoon. He wasn't sure what to make of his reaction to her. He could still see the sadness in her coffee-colored eyes. Her vulnerability made him feel as though he needed to protect her, even though he barely knew her.

Since she'd moved to town more than two years ago with her husband and children, Nathan had seen her on occasion at church, but their paths had rarely crossed. He'd never paid much attention to her before, but the attractive young widow certainly had his attention now.

Nathan strode across the lobby and gazed outside. Melanie was already out of sight, but she wasn't out of his thoughts. She had her hands full with those live-wire boys. With a smile, he remembered his own childhood. He'd been exactly like them—full of mischief and always fighting with his older brother Marcus, who was now an investment banker in New

York City. Or maybe a more accurate description was trying to compete with him. Wasn't he still trying to compete with Marcus? Their father was always bragging about some big deal that Marcus had closed. Nathan wanted that kind of attention. But he didn't want to think about that. He'd rather think about the lovely widow.

Nathan felt an obligation to help her in whatever way he could, because single parents had double duty. Despite her attempt to put on a brave face, he could see that she was still struggling with her grief. What must a person go through when someone close to them died, especially a spouse? He had no idea. No one close to him had ever died. His parents, both sets of grandparents, brother and sister were still living. Yet, Melanie believed that he understood.

Wishing he knew more about her, Nathan stared out the glass doors toward the Kellerville town square where the courthouse stood. A gazebo graced the expansive lawn in front. As he stood there, the clock in the tower chimed four times. He supposed he should get back to work, but he couldn't get Melanie off his mind. Maybe he should talk to his cousin Juliane. She and her husband Lukas babysat Melanie's boys occasionally. Could Juliane shed any light on the young widow?

With a heavy sigh, Nathan turned toward his office. Then he spied Trudy Becker, who had given Melanie and her boys a rather disdainful look when they left the bank. She'd given the same look to him and his brother Marcus when they'd been kids. He hadn't liked it then and he didn't like it now. Her expression prompted him not to wait, but to find out more about Melanie today.

Nathan marched over to the loan officer's desk. "Trudy, I have some personal business I have to take care of away from the bank. If anyone needs me, you can reach me on my cell."

Not waiting for any comment from Trudy, Nathan left the bank. He hardly ever left the bank, especially for personal reasons, and he enjoyed seeing the speculation in Trudy's expression. He hated having bad thoughts about people, but the woman was sometimes unpleasant to be around. He often wondered why his father had hired her, but she'd been there since he was a kid. He hoped by the time he took over as president of the bank that she would be retired.

As Nathan crossed the square, he shook unpleasant thoughts from his head. He wanted to enjoy the beautiful spring day in this little southwestern Ohio town, where he'd grown up.

Quickening his step, he passed the gazebo surrounded by a rainbow of tulips. He headed straight across the square to Keller's Variety, where Juliane worked for her father as manager. When he entered the store, the smell of potpourri and leather goods greeted him. Looking around, he spied Juliane as she helped a customer.

While he waited, he perused the merchandise that ranged from knickknacks to specialty clothing. "Variety" was definitely a good name for the store that his uncle Ray owned.

After the customer left the store, Juliane came his way. "Hi, Nathan. I'm surprised to see you here. What are you shopping for today?"

"Information. Do you have time to talk?"

Curiosity painting her face, Juliane glanced around the store. "No customers at the moment, so I guess so. What kind of information do you need?"

"Information about Melanie Drake?"

Juliane raised her eyebrows. "So you finally have a romantic interest—"

"Absolutely not. This is strictly business."

Juliane chuckled. "I should've known. My nose-to-the-grindstone cousin doesn't have time for romance. He's in love with the bank."

"You're right. I love that bank. It's what gets me up in the morning and makes my day." Nathan knew his response would get a rise out of Juliane, but his life *did* revolve around work.

In the past few years, his dad had taken more and more time off as his parents did a little globetrotting. He left Nathan in charge. He knew this was his father's way of testing him—to see whether he could run the bank. And Nathan intended to show his father that the bank would be in good hands when he retired.

"You're no fun to tease." Juliane swatted at him with one hand. "So why do you want to know about Melanie?"

Nathan wondered how he could get a handle on Melanie's life without divulging her reason for coming into the bank. He'd have to keep his statements as vague as possible. "She was in the bank today with her two boys."

"So what do you want to know?"

"How's she doing? She seemed a little…ah…I guess you'd say lost."

"Lost? Still grieving, maybe, but not lost." Grimacing, Juliane shook her head. "I thought she was doing better. Do you think she isn't?"

"I don't know. I sensed that she might feel a little overwhelmed with having to raise those boys by herself."

"I'm sure it's been hard without Tim. I should have been better about checking on her, but we haven't visited as much since she went back to work." Juliane sighed. "Maybe you should ask her out."

"Don't get any crazy ideas."

"Come on. It would do you both good. You need some social life, and she'd probably like some adult conversation outside of work at least one evening a week."

Nathan shook his head. "Don't try to play matchmaker,

Juliane. I'm the last person she needs to date. After what she went through with her husband, she probably isn't looking for another man with a health problem."

"Come on. It's been at least two years since you've had a flare-up with your Crohn's disease."

Nathan dropped his gaze. He didn't want her to guess that he'd had a couple of flare-ups that she didn't know about. Keeping his health problems to himself was the way he liked to operate. He quietly sought treatment and definitely didn't broadcast his difficulties. He knew the stress from work caused some of his problem, but work was what he lived for. "Are you forgetting that I've already been through one broken relationship because of it? I don't need to have another one."

"I haven't forgotten, but Andrea didn't deserve a good man like you. She was selfish and spoiled. I'm glad she broke up with you."

"Wow! I had no idea you liked her so much."

"Quit being sarcastic." Juliane gave him an annoyed look. "You know she did you a favor by dumping you. You'd have been miserable being married to that…that—"

"Drop it. It's history. Besides, I like my single life."

Juliane laid a hand on Nathan's arm. "I'm sorry I was grousing about your old girlfriend, but she treated you shabbily."

"Let's not talk about her."

"Okay." Juliane brightened. "Let's talk about Melanie instead."

Nathan narrowed his gaze. "Juliane."

"I thought that's why you came to see me."

"I did, but I didn't expect that you'd start with this matchmaking." Nathan sighed. "So what do you think about getting her boys involved in the youth baseball league? They are so full of energy, so I thought playing baseball would be a good outlet for their liveliness. Has she ever mentioned signing them up?"

"Not that I recall?" Juliane gave him a puzzled look. "You mean you had to ask me whether you can recruit her kids for the bank's youth baseball team?"

"No." Nathan frowned. He had no idea he would invite Juliane's matchmaking with his inquiry about Melanie and her kids. "I wanted to make sure she wouldn't think I was interfering if I suggested the baseball for them. Also, I was just wondering how you think she's doing these days."

Juliane chuckled. "I don't know about the baseball, but now that I've had a chance to think more about the two of you together, I like the idea."

"Well, I don't. So stop."

Juliane gave him a Cheshire-cat grin. "Okay. If you say so."

"Would she be receptive to a little help with her kids?"

"You'll have to find that out for yourself. I can't help you with that, but I can help you if you'd like to ask her out."

"I won't be asking for that kind of help."

The bell over the door jangled as a woman entered the store. *Saved by the bell*. The old cliché couldn't have been more appropriate.

"We'll see." Juliane hurried off to wait on the customer. "Remember what I said."

"I'm sure you'll remind me. I'll talk to you later." Annoyed, Nathan left the store and moseyed across the square toward the bank. His visit with Juliane had not gone as he'd planned. She not only didn't give him any clue about Melanie's state of mind, but Juliane had started that whole dating scenario. That was the last thing he wanted.

How was he going to get the answers he needed when even Juliane, who was as close to Melanie as anyone, didn't seem to know what was going on with her? He wanted to help her, especially with her boys. From what he'd seen, they needed a male influence. He still wasn't sure whether Melanie would think he was interfering unnecessarily if he interjected himself into her sons' lives. Did he dare take a chance and ask?

Chapter Two

The following Friday night, Melanie walked across the parking lot toward the clubhouse at the Kellerville Country Club. The sun sat just above the trees lining the first fairway on the golf course. Before she reached the door, Nathan, wearing the suit he'd probably worn to work, came out to meet her. Unlike his suit, the white and hot pink scrubs she'd worn to work weren't exactly country-club attire, but she hadn't had time to change. He smiled, but even his smile didn't ease the nervous tension in her shoulders.

"Hi, thanks for coming." He opened the door for her.

"I should be thanking you." After stepping into the lobby, she stopped in front of the round dark oak table decorated with a floral centerpiece of white hydrangeas and lilies.

"Let's both thank Juliane and Lukas for watching Ryan and Andrew tonight."

Melanie nodded. "The boys are so excited Juliane and Lukas are taking them to the Dairy Barn, then to the movies. They practically pushed me out the door so the fun could begin."

Nathan chuckled. "I think Lukas was more excited than your boys. He told me he wanted to see that movie, but he thought people would look at him strangely if he went to a kids' movie without any kids. He was glad to borrow your boys for the evening."

"Lukas never mentioned that." As the tension in her shoulders dissipated, Melanie realized that Nathan seemed to have a knack for putting her at ease—at least for the moment.

"Don't tell him I let his secret slip." Nathan gestured to his right. "This way. I reserved one of the small meeting rooms, so we'll have some privacy."

"Okay."

"Do you want to work while we eat, or eat first, then go over what I have to show you?"

"What do you think?" Melanie hoped Nathan would take the lead.

"If you aren't in a rush, let's eat, then work. We can do the buffet. It's always good."

"Okay." Melanie liked that Nathan was taking charge. Tim had been that way.

After entering the room, Nathan laid the folder she'd given him on the table. Then he held out a chair for her at one of the three square tables covered with white tablecloths. "Please have a seat while I let someone know we're here. After they take our drink orders, we can go through the buffet line."

"Okay." As Nathan left the room Melanie sighed. He must think she had a one-word vocabulary. Even though the tension in her shoulders had eased, now she seemed to be tongue-tied. Why did he make her feel so awkward?

When Juliane had first suggested that Melanie meet Nathan at the country club for their discussion, she'd thought Juliane was trying to do a little matchmaking. But, so far, Nathan was all about business. Melanie decided she was being paranoid to think otherwise. She reminded herself that this wasn't a date. It was a business meeting.

After Melanie and Nathan got their food, they ate quietly for several minutes. Sneaking a peek at Nathan, she wondered whether he was naturally a quiet person or whether he wasn't interested in talking with her. The silence made her anxious. He made her anxious. Everything about this meeting made her anxious.

"Do you like living in Kellerville?"

Nathan's question startled Melanie. She took a minute to collect her thoughts. "Yeah."

"Your hesitation makes me think that wasn't a resounding endorsement. You don't have to tell me you like it here if you don't."

"Oh, but I do like it. Kellerville is the first place I've ever felt at home."

Nathan knit his eyebrows. "Really?"

"Really. Have you always lived here?"

"My whole life—except the years I was in college. And then I was only an hour's drive away in Cincinnati. Even though almost everyone in town knows all the good and bad things I've done in my life, I enjoy living here. I like having extended family around—grandparents, aunts, uncles and cousins—people who love me, despite my flaws. There's no other place I'd rather be." Nathan broke apart a roll and slathered it with butter. "Did you consider moving closer to your family after your husband died?"

Taking a sip of water, Melanie thought about her response. If she told him about her upbringing, would he think less of her? What would he say if he knew she'd spent most of her childhood in an array of foster homes because her mother couldn't kick her drug habit—the habit that eventually killed her? Could he understand how she felt about never knowing her father? "I don't have any family."

The furrows between his eyebrows deepened. "No parents? No siblings?"

Melanie nodded. At this point, she wished she were an orphan. "That's right. I grew up in foster care."

"Oh." Nathan shook his head. "I sure stuck my foot in my mouth, rambling on about extended family and all, didn't I?"

"That's okay. You didn't know." Shaking her head, Melanie smiled halfheartedly. While she finished her meal, Melanie's thoughts wandered. What would it be like to have Nathan's life—a life of privilege, love and family?

She shouldn't be envious, but she was. She and Tim had been well on their way to building a stable, happy home when everything had fallen apart. A few months after Tim had died, everyone else's life had seemed to go back to normal, but hers hadn't. Despite the help of her grief recovery group, she'd let herself get stuck in the past. This meeting with Nathan was a part of getting unstuck and moving forward.

The impending trip to see Tim's parents had finally prompted her to seek advice on some investment strategies. She didn't want to give them another reason to disapprove of her. Her finances weren't any of their business, but she knew Tim's father would insist that she give an accounting for the boys' sake. She didn't know how to refuse. Her upcoming trip to see them hung in her thoughts like a heavy weight.

Nathan pushed his plate aside and picked up the folder. "Are you ready to tackle this financial stuff?"

"Sure." Melanie hoped Nathan couldn't read the uncertainty in her voice.

First, Nathan went through the charts and graphs that he'd prepared showing her where her money was now. Then he explained more charts that gave her several scenarios for her investments. She was having a hard time concentrating because his strong-looking hand distracted her as it moved across the papers. Besides, she didn't know anything about stocks or bonds or mutual funds. His talk about asset allocations, alternative investments, derivatives and diversification still had her head swimming even though he had tried to explain them in terms she could understand. She'd grown up without money, so she'd let Tim deal with that kind of stuff. Now she had to change her thinking.

Finally, when Nathan finished, he looked up at her. "What do you think?"

"I need time to look this over more."

"Wise decision." Smiling, he nodded and handed her the folder. "Study this. Then we can meet here again next Friday. Working together, we can create a great investment plan for you and your boys."

Standing, Melanie nodded. "I wonder whether Juliane and Lukas would babysit again?"

"I'll make sure they do."

"I don't want to be a pest." Melanie started for the door.

"They're not going to think you're a pest." Nathan reached out and touched her arm. "One thing before you go. Are Ryan and Andrew signed up for the youth baseball league?"

Trying to ignore the way his touch made her pulse quicken, Melanie shook her head. "No, I haven't signed them up. Isn't it too late for that? I thought practices started last month."

"Yeah, for the older kids. The younger leagues don't start practice until school's out."

"So it's not too late then?"

"That's right. I work with them because their season is shorter, which works out better with my schedule at the bank. We try to keep the younger kids in a more low-key atmosphere. We want them to have fun and learn the basics—not worry so much about winning or losing," Nathan explained as he accompanied her to the lobby.

Melanie shrugged. "I don't know. They haven't been very well-behaved lately."

"Maybe that's another reason to sign them up. They need to expend some of that extra energy."

Melanie nodded. "That's a good thought. I'll ask them if they'd like to play."

"Super! If you'd like, I'll help you get them registered."

"Thanks. I appreciate that."

"I'll walk you to your car." As Nathan started to open the door for Melanie, a man called Nathan's name. He turned to look. "Hey, Gerry. I'm just finishing up here. I'll be with you in a minute."

When Nathan turned back to her, Melanie shook her head. "You've got another meeting, so go ahead. I can see myself out, and I'll see you next Friday."

"You're sure?"

Melanie nodded. "I am. I'll tell the boys about baseball."

"Okay. Have a good night."

"Good night." Melanie tried to tell herself she wasn't disappointed that Nathan had so quickly abandoned the idea of escorting her to her car. She reminded herself that he was a prominent man in this community—a very busy man. After she'd mourned her husband for two years, why had Nathan suddenly caught her attention? She wasn't sure what to make of her feelings or whether they were a good thing. Had his kindness and concern for her and her boys opened up her grieving heart?

When Melanie arrived home, lights glowed in the windows of her two-story house that sat on a hillside on the edge of Kellerville. Juliane and Lukas's car was parked in the driveway. Melanie remembered how excited Tim and she had been as they purchased this home with its big backyard for the boys and lots of room inside. Before they had moved to Kellerville, they had lived in a tiny old house with no yard. This house was their dream home. She hadn't thought of that in months. Maybe the financial talk had brought that memory to mind.

Lots of memories—happy and sad—had flooded her thoughts tonight.

As she opened the front door, she forced herself to think about the future, not the past. Stepping into the front hall, she closed the door behind her. Before she could completely gather her thoughts, Ryan and Andrew raced out of the den to greet her. They talked over each other about the movie as they vied for her attention.

Melanie looked over at Juliane, who stood behind the boys. "I guess they enjoyed the movie."

"I did, too." Chuckling, Lukas put an arm around Juliane's shoulders as he joined them. "Juliane just enjoyed the popcorn."

"Thanks so much for taking them. I can't tell you how much I appreciate it."

"We loved doing it." Juliane gave the boys a hug.

Ryan and Andrew tugged on Lukas's arm. "Come on, Lukas. Let's finish our game."

"Duty calls. Besides, I'm winning." Lukas gave the women a helpless grin.

As Lukas followed the boys back to the den, Juliane turned to Melanie. "He's just a big kid at heart."

Melanie couldn't help thinking of how that description could also apply to Nathan. He had video games on his computer at the bank and had let Ryan and Andrew play one of them. Plus, his face had lit up when he'd talked about youth baseball. It was clear that the program meant a lot to him. She didn't want to be thinking about Nathan, but he was front and center in her mind.

Melanie waved the folder Nathan had given her in the air. "I have to go over this. Then Nathan and I are meeting again on Friday."

Juliane patted Melanie's arm. "Lukas and I will be willing

to watch your boys again on Friday, especially if you want to go on a date."

"Thanks, but this isn't a date. It's business. Besides, I don't see myself doing any dating. Even if someone did ask me out, I'm not ready yet." Even as she said the words, Melanie wondered whether they were true.

What would she say if Nathan asked her for a date? She would say no. Her boys were her focus. She didn't have time for dates. So she pushed thoughts of Nathan away before they could settle in her mind.

Thankfully, Juliane dropped the subject as they made their way toward the kitchen. Their conversation turned to work and church activities. By the time Lukas had finished playing the game with the boys, Melanie was satisfied that Juliane wouldn't bring up the subject of dating again.

After Juliane and Lukas left, Melanie sat on the couch in the living room while the boys watched TV in the den. As she sat in the quiet room, Juliane's suggestion about dating popped back into her mind, and Melanie couldn't help thinking about her evening with Nathan. He came from a prominent family in his hometown and knew about money and the finer things in life. He was like Tim.

But she'd never been able to please Tim's parents, Harlan and Georgia Drake, and their displeasure hadn't stopped when Tim died. They constantly complained about the way she was raising Ryan and Andrew. She feared even thinking about dating because they would probably disapprove of her seeing another man.

Melanie didn't know why these thoughts about Nathan were running through her head. She had to blame them on Juliane because Nathan had given her absolutely no indication that he was interested in anything beyond their business dealings and signing her boys up for baseball.

Melanie picked up the framed photograph from the end

table next to the couch. She stared at it. Tim's smiling face looked back at her. "Tim, I miss you so much, but I know I have to move on and start living for the future. The boys need me to be strong."

"Mom, who are you talking to?"

Melanie glanced up to find Ryan standing in the doorway, Andrew close behind him. The boys looked so much like Tim with their dark brown hair and eyes. Wondering whether they could understand, she placed the photograph back on the end table. As she motioned for them to join her on the couch, she gave them a sheepish grin. "You caught me talking to your dad, or at least his photo."

"Mom, are you sad?" Andrew sat beside her.

Ryan sat on the other side of her. "Don't cry, Mom."

"I'm not going to cry." Melanie put her arms around her sons' shoulders and squeezed them.

"But I hear you crying sometimes." Ryan snuggled close.

"I won't be sad tonight." Melanie sighed. She hated that her little boys had heard her crying. Their lives should be carefree. They shouldn't have to worry about their mother, but sometimes the loneliness just closed around her and made her ache inside.

Ryan jumped up from the couch and looked at her with fierce determination. "I'll take care of you, Mom. I'll make you happy."

"Me, too. I'll help you not be sad." Andrew reached over and hugged her tight.

Not to be outdone, Ryan joined in the hug. "Dad wouldn't want us to be sad. He'd want us to be happy, right?"

"That's right." Fighting back tears for a whole different reason than sadness, Melanie held out her hand. "Let's make a promise to be happy."

"Good idea, Mom." Nodding, Ryan put his hand on top of hers.

"Me, too." Andrew put on a brave smile and put his hand on top of Ryan's.

After they stacked their hands, Melanie looked at her sons. "What should we say?"

"You tell us, Mom," Andrew said.

"Let's say that we promise to help each other be happy."

"Okay," the boys chorused, then repeated the phrase along with Melanie.

Melanie hugged them. "I think we should pray about it."

Ryan pointed at himself. "Let me pray."

"Okay."

Andrew tapped her on the arm. "Can I pray, too?"

"We can all pray." Melanie grasped their hands, and each of them said a prayer.

After they finished praying, Melanie remembered Nathan's suggestion about youth baseball. She realized that she hadn't thought about getting the boys involved in the baseball league because the last two years had been about surviving—getting past Tim's death. Now she had to start living again for the future—for her boys and for herself. In addition to getting her financial dealings in order, she would work doubly hard to look at the positive. She would remember that God had a plan for her life.

"Can we stay up to play one more game?" Ryan stared at her with expectation.

"Okay, but before you leave, I have something I want to tell you." Melanie scooted forward on the couch. "Mr. Keller, from the bank, asked if you were interested in playing in the youth baseball league after school is out for the summer. What do you think?"

"We don't have gloves and stuff." Andrew's little face scrunched up with concern.

"We'll get what you need." Melanie patted him on the head.

"Yeah, Andrew, it'll be lots of fun. I'll help you learn to bat." Ryan's little chest puffed out.

Melanie held back a smile at Ryan's bravado. "So does that mean I should tell Mr. Keller to sign you up?"

"Yeah. Can we get the stuff we need tomorrow?" Without waiting for Melanie's answer, Ryan turned to Andrew. "We can practice tomorrow after we get everything."

"We'll go shopping after I get off work."

Ryan and Andrew cheered as they raced back to the den. For once they weren't fighting. They were actually assisting each other. Her heart swelled with pride at their bravery in wanting to make life easier for her. They were so much like their dad—so fervent in their desire to take care of her. Tim had always been there to help her tackle every problem. He stood beside her and protected her against anyone who would try to bring her down, especially his own parents.

But Tim wasn't here, so she had to confront her own problems and stand up to his parents by herself. That battle couldn't involve the boys. They needed to have the love of their only set of grandparents. Ryan and Andrew needed that connection to their father.

Melanie wondered whether she'd be able to keep the promise to be happy. Taking a deep breath, she vowed to honor it. She had a lot of things to tackle—making a decision about the finances, giving her boys a good measure of discipline and dealing with Tim's parents in a loving way. One new problem had presented itself. Nathan Keller. After she'd gotten over her initial nervousness, he'd seemed so easy to talk to. How was she going to handle her unexpected attraction to him?

Chapter Three

Holding his BlackBerry in his hand, Nathan paced back and forth across the clubhouse lobby. Melanie should have been here by now. It was well past six o'clock, the appointed meeting time. Maybe she was running late at work. Should he call his uncle's office to find out? Dismissing the idea, Nathan decided to wait a few more minutes.

As Nathan continued to pace, he wondered whether Melanie would arrive in her scrubs again. He had to admit that she'd looked good even in scrubs. Ever since she'd called him at the bank to say that her boys wanted to play baseball, he couldn't quit thinking about her. He couldn't deny his fascination with her, but he cautioned himself against any romantic ideas.

The door opened and Melanie rushed into the lobby, almost running into him. She stopped short when she saw him. "I'm so sorry to be late. Dr. Joe had a last-minute emergency today, and I had to stay late."

"No problem." Taking in her lime-green scrubs covered with little toothbrushes, he gestured toward the hallway leading to the meeting rooms. She looked good in those, too. "We've got the same room as last week."

Melanie took a deep breath and fell into step beside him. "I should've gotten your cell number, so I could've called."

"Don't worry about it." Nathan pulled out a chair for her, then sat on the chair perpendicular to hers. "I know what it's like to work late."

She pulled the financial folder he'd given her and some other papers out of her satchel. She set the folder on the table, then held out the papers. "These are the paperwork and fees for the baseball league."

"Thanks. I'm glad Ryan and Andrew want to participate."

"They are so excited about getting to play, although I think Andrew is a little nervous. But he won't admit it because he doesn't want his big brother to think he's a wimp."

"I could give them a little practice with the fundamentals of baseball." Even as the words left his mouth, he couldn't believe he was saying them. Had he just volunteered to help her kids? He'd thought all along about helping them, but when was he going to have time to do it, especially when he had to make sure his people were ready for the upcoming bank audit? Her pretty face must have fried his brain.

She placed a hand over her heart. "Thank you. That would be wonderful! We bought equipment the other day, but I couldn't help them play. I was never very good at sports."

After hearing Melanie's statement, Nathan knew he was doing the right thing whether he had time or not. He would have to make time. Those little boys needed a man in their lives. But he cautioned himself against getting involved with Melanie. He would make time for the boys, but he didn't have time for a woman in his life.

Nathan stood. "Let's get our food."

"Good. I'm starved. We were so busy today that I barely had time for lunch."

"I'll have to tell Uncle Joe not to work you so hard." Nathan grabbed a plate.

"Oh, don't do that. Dr. Joe's a wonderful boss. He's so good about giving me flexible work hours to accommodate my boys' schedules. I wouldn't want to complain."

"Melanie, I was only kidding." Nathan chuckled.

"Oh. I guess I should've known that anyone who has video games on his office computer is someone who isn't always serious." Melanie grimaced. "You always seemed so…"

"So what?"

"So formal, at least when I've seen you at church."

"I'll have to show you more of my informal side." Nathan laughed halfheartedly, wondering how or when he planned to do that.

He wanted to kick himself as Melanie ducked her head and concentrated on getting her food. He could see that he'd embarrassed her—something he'd never intended. Tonight she'd seemed so much more relaxed than the last time they'd met—talking about her boys and telling him she was starved—until he'd said the wrong thing. Now she wouldn't even look at him. Could he find a way to undo his blunder?

Without saying a word, they walked back to their meeting room. Nathan hoped they could somehow recapture their earlier camaraderie. After he said a blessing for the food, they began eating in silence. Finally, he decided that he'd been thinking too much about himself instead of thinking about Melanie. That was his problem. He had to get Melanie to talk about herself. Or better yet, her boys. He knew no mother could resist the chance to talk about her kids.

"So what do Juliane and Lukas have planned for your boys tonight?"

Melanie looked at him for the first time since his bad attempt at a joke. "They're staying at the house and watching some videos I picked up."

"Lukas must not have had any kids' movies he wanted to see."

"Unless he wanted to see the ones I rented." Melanie smiled.

Her smile tugged at his heart and made him want things he shouldn't want. She was here for a business matter and nothing more. A man with his health problems was the last thing she needed in her life right now, anyway. He had to keep that firmly in mind, but he couldn't help himself. He still wanted to know all about her. "Who takes care of Ryan and Andrew when school is out in the summer?"

"The rec center has a summer day camp that the boys attend for several weeks. And they usually spend a couple of weeks with Tim's parents. Otherwise, Barbara Keller watches them. Sometimes a teenage girl in our neighborhood babysits, but she's not always reliable. She's the one who was supposed to watch them the day I had to bring them to the bank."

"I had no idea my aunt Barbara watched your boys." Nathan wondered where he'd been that he didn't know this.

Sure, the past two years at the bank had been crazy with the financial markets going up and down like a roller coaster. He'd worked long hours and socialized little, but that was no excuse for being completely oblivious to things going on around him. Was it time for a change?

"Ryan and Andrew love Barbara. She's wonderful with them."

"Yeah. Aunt Barbara was always lots of fun when I was growing up, too."

While they continued eating, Nathan thought about this aunt and his huge extended family and the love they shared, and tried to imagine what it would be like to grow up without a father. His dad had always been demanding, but he was fair and a good example. He'd always taught Nathan that he could do or be anything he wanted. Having someone who believed in him gave him confidence to tackle life's hard choices.

Nathan wanted to follow in his father's footsteps and one

day be president of the bank. That's why he worked so hard—
to please his dad. Every boy should have a man to look up to.
Could he be that kind of example for Melanie's boys without
involving himself in her life? That would be a delicate balancing act.

When they finished eating, Nathan picked up the folder
lying on the table. "Are you ready to undertake this?"

Melanie smiled, but uncertainty radiated from her eyes. "I
wish I could be sure that I'm making the right decision about
this. That's why I've put it off for so long. If I mess up with
Tim's money, I'll have to answer to his parents."

Nathan tried not to frown. "But it's your money."

"I know, but they believe I might not use it wisely, so it'll
be there for Ryan and Andrew. In fact, Tim's dad kept hinting that I should let him invest it for me." Shaking her head,
Melanie sighed. "I didn't want to get entangled in that setup,
so I've been stalling."

Nathan nodded. "I think you're right to steer away from a
scenario like that. It's better to have a neutral party help with
an investment strategy."

"Thanks. I didn't know how to tell Mr. Drake that I'd rather
not have his help. So now that you're developing an investment
portfolio for me, I can show him it's being taken care of. If I
messed up these investments, the Drakes would like me even
less than they do now."

"You mean you don't get along with Tim's parents?"

"Unfortunately, that's correct. They weren't happy when
Tim and I eloped." She nodded as a sad little smile curved
her mouth—a very kissable mouth.

Trouble. He was in trouble with a capital *T.* Here she was
talking about how she'd eloped, and he was thinking about
kissing her. He shouldn't be thinking that at all. He quickly
opened the folder and tried to concentrate on it rather than

on her kissable lips. "Were they just unhappy about the elopement?"

"No. They were unhappy about the whole marriage. Tim and I came from two different worlds, and his parents were sure he'd made a mistake when he married me, especially since I was so young—barely nineteen. They don't even approve of me now." Melanie sighed. "The anniversary of the day I met Tim is coming up, and that's always a hard time for me."

She mentioned the date, and he frowned. "Elise and Seth are getting married that day."

Melanie nodded at the mention of his cousin's name. "I know. I'm just hoping I can make it through their wedding without crying."

Nathan couldn't understand Tim's parents. How could anyone not adore Melanie Drake? Glancing up, Nathan didn't miss the determined set of her shoulders. He thought about telling her that people always cried at weddings, so her tears wouldn't seem unusual. But that would be a rather unsympathetic statement. He didn't need to put his foot in his mouth again tonight. "That has to be tough."

"Yeah, but I'll survive. If I can survive Tim's parents, I can make it through Elise and Seth's wedding. Besides, as I said, Barbara's been so kind to me. I can't imagine missing her youngest daughter's wedding." Melanie's eyes held a faraway look. "Tim was always so good to me. I know it was hard for him to be torn between his parents and me, but he always took my side."

"I have confidence that you'll do fine at the wedding."

"Yes, I will." She leaned forward. "Let's go over this financial stuff."

"Do you have any questions?"

"Tons." She spread the different plans on the table in front of her, then looked up at him. "Here's the deal. I was in charge of the household budget and paid the bills, but Tim did the investing and stuff like that. He'd ask me for my input, but I didn't know anything about investments, so I always let him make the decisions. Maybe I should've been more involved, then I wouldn't be so lost now."

"Tell me what you want to know."

She stared at him, as if she was trying to formulate her questions. Her wavy dark hair was pulled away from her face and held at the back of her head with a clip. A few strands had escaped and fallen across her cheek. He was tempted to reach over and push them behind her ear. He clenched the pen in his hand to keep from acting on the thought.

Finally, she cleared her throat and tapped one of the papers. "I'm interested in this plan, but I'd like more information about it. The returns look promising, but I think the risk might be higher than I'm comfortable with. Which one do you like the best? And what would happen if I didn't do anything and left everything just as I have it now?"

"You've given this a lot of thought, haven't you?"

"And prayer."

"Very wise." Nathan knew that he often didn't make his decisions a matter of prayer. He needed to take a lesson from Melanie. She was seeking his advice, but he was learning from her instead. "Do you mind taking a little personality test that'll help determine the kind of investment strategy that you might feel most comfortable with?"

"Should I have done that before?"

Nathan shook his head. "I feel it's better to have a grasp of what's available first, so you understand what to expect. Then, this will give you a little more information to help you decide."

"Okay. Sounds good."

For the next hour Nathan walked Melanie through the personality test, then helped her make some decisions about short- and long-term investments. He learned a lot more about the woman who was making him rethink his priorities. He watched her as she laughed at some of the test questions and studied the plans again with great intensity. She had an almost old-fashioned beauty. In spite of the scrubs she wore, she looked as if she'd stepped out of the past. She reminded him of a photograph of his grandmother when she was a young woman.

For the moment, Nathan was glad to be the man she needed to answer her questions, but he realized he had no hope of ever living up to Tim Drake. Nathan knew he should remember that when he thought of things like kissing her or asking her to be his date for Elise and Seth's wedding.

"Mom, when is Mr. Keller going to get here?" Ryan pounded his fist into his new baseball glove as he stood in the front yard.

"He said he'd try to get here around three o'clock, but you must remember he is a very busy man. He has an important job at the bank and sometimes has to work on Saturday." Taking in the warmth of the sun, Melanie pulled on the bill of Ryan's baseball cap. "I had to work this morning, too."

"See what I can do?" Ryan tossed a baseball into the air, then caught it in his glove.

"I can do that, too." Andrew grabbed a ball and imitated his brother. "Mine went higher."

"No, it didn't. Mine was higher." Ryan threw his ball into the air again. "See."

Feeling a little headache start, Melanie rubbed her temples. She couldn't have the boys battling each other when Nathan was here. "Boys, if you act like that while Mr. Keller is here, that'll be the end of any baseball practice. Do you understand?"

Both boys hung their heads. "Yes, ma'am."

"Good." Melanie picked up one of the baseballs and tossed it from hand to hand. "We'll practice catching while we wait."

Ryan pounded his glove again. "I hope he gets here soon."

Me, too. Melanie told herself that she wasn't sure why that thought had popped into her brain, but she had to admit she wasn't being truthful. She did know why her thoughts echoed Ryan's. Nathan had been on her mind since their initial meeting at the bank, and especially after their meetings at the country club.

He'd had her attention from the moment he'd shown the boys the video game and winked at her as he'd asked her to keep their secret. It was a pleasure to see a man who was so good with kids—especially a man with such a wonderful mischievous smile. But she couldn't let herself dwell on that. She had to temper her thoughts with some common sense and look at the whole thing logically. Nathan was coming over to help Ryan and Andrew. His conversation last night clearly indicated that his only mission, besides giving her financial advice, was helping the boys get ready to play baseball. Besides, her first priority was always her boys, and a new relationship would only get in the way.

With those thoughts at the forefront of her mind, she took turns tossing the ball to Ryan, then to Andrew. After several minutes of that exercise, Ryan picked up the metal bat that lay on the driveway. "Let's do some batting."

"I think we should wait for Mr. Keller." Melanie held out her hand for the bat.

Reluctantly, Ryan handed it to her, his mouth forming a pout. "He's probably not going to come at all."

"He'll be here soon." Despite trying to reassure Ryan, Melanie wondered whether Nathan might not show. Surely if he couldn't make it, he would call. If he failed to contact her at all, her opinion of him would definitely change. Maybe that's exactly what she needed in order to keep herself from thinking about him too much. But she didn't want her sons to be disappointed. They'd already been through enough.

"I'm not waiting anymore. Baseball's a dumb game anyway." Ryan threw his glove on the ground and stomped up the walk to the front door.

As Ryan looked back to check on her reaction, Melanie forced herself to remain calm. "If that's the way you feel, then you can go inside. Andrew and I will keep playing a little catch until Mr. Keller gets here."

Andrew gave Ryan a superior look before he held up his glove. "Okay, Mom. Throw me the ball."

"Get ready." Out of the corner of her eye, she could see Ryan vacillating about his decision as he held open the door.

Suspecting that Ryan didn't want his little brother to get any attention that he wasn't getting, she tossed the ball to Andrew.

While Melanie waited for Andrew to throw the ball back, sadness seeped into her heart again. She didn't want the boys to fight. Why couldn't everything be like it was before Tim died when they were a loving happy family? Catching the ball, she remembered the promise she'd made with Ryan and Andrew, and she pledged not to let the sadness win.

As she got ready to toss the ball to Andrew again, a metallic-blue SUV turned onto their street and slowed down. She didn't know what kind of vehicle Nathan drove, but she held her breath and hoped for her kids' sake that Nathan was behind the wheel. The car drew closer. Her heart did a little flip-flop when she recognized Nathan in the driver's seat.

"He's here!" Ryan raced back into the yard and picked up his glove.

Melanie looked at him. "Change your mind?"

Not meeting her gaze, Ryan nodded.

"What do you have to say for yourself?"

He pounded his glove. "I'm sorry."

"Okay. Let's not have any more temper tantrums."

After nodding again, Ryan raced away to join Andrew, who was already showing Nathan his new glove. While the boys clamored for Nathan's attention, he cast a glance in her direction and smiled. Smiling in return, she tried to calm her racing pulse as she joined them.

"Hi." He grinned. "I'm sorry I'm late. Work, but you know how that goes. I would've been on time, but I had to go home and change."

"I understand." Melanie took in Nathan's jeans, gray T-shirt with the Cincinnati Reds emblem on the front and his sneakers. His casual side was just as good-looking as the formal one. She had to think about something else. "Do you want to go into the backyard?"

"Yeah, that way we won't have to chase any balls into the street." Nathan grabbed a couple of bats and started toward the back of the house.

The boys raced ahead. Having regained her equilibrium, Melanie fell into step beside Nathan. "Thanks for coming. This means a lot to Ryan and Andrew. I hope I got them the right equipment. I bought the stuff that the guy at the sporting goods store recommended."

Nathan held up the bat. "This will work fine."

"I had no idea kids' bats were so expensive. But now that you're my financial advisor, I guess I can afford to buy a couple."

Nathan chuckled. "So you still feel good about the investment strategy you picked out?"

"I do until I think about explaining it to Tim's parents."

"I'm going to prepare a file for you with everything laid out, so you can easily explain it to them." Nathan stopped and looked at her. "And if you want, I'll be glad to help you talk to them."

Melanie shook her head. "You shouldn't have to deal with them. They're not your problem."

"If you ever need me, I'll be there."

Melanie knew he meant that in a business sense, but her thoughts strayed into personal territory. Not good. Not good at all. Explaining to Tim's parents what she'd done with their son's money was bad enough. Trying to explain a new relationship would be even worse. She had to concentrate on being a good mother and forget any thoughts of a personal life of her own. She had no room for another man in her life. Her sons, church and work were enough to keep her life busy and fulfilled.

While Melanie sat on the deck at the back of the house, Nathan showed Ryan and Andrew how to hold and swing the bat. Then he tossed a few practice pitches. Ryan did well, but Andrew struggled. Although the boys were only a year apart in age, Andrew was smaller than most seven-year-old boys. He tried to keep up with his big brother, but he had a hard time. And lately Ryan didn't make things easier for his brother.

Nathan's patience, as he worked with Andrew, amazed Melanie and made her want to discard all those doubts about her personal life. She reminded herself that Nathan was here for the boys, not her.

"Okay, guys, let's see if you can field some balls that I hit."

"I get to go first." Ryan pounded a fist into his glove.

"There's no going first or last. It'll all depend on where I happen to hit the ball." Nathan picked up one of the bats. "We'll do some fly balls and some ground balls. You guys need to be ready for whatever comes to you."

"I'm ready." Imitating his brother, Andrew smacked his glove.

Nathan quickly made some makeshift bases and had the boys position themselves as if they were playing infield positions. "Okay, here comes the first ball."

As the ball skimmed along the ground toward Andrew, he put his glove down to catch it. When he successfully captured the ball in the glove, he grinned and looked toward Nathan for approval. "I did it."

"Good job, Andrew. Now toss the ball to Ryan." Nathan motioned toward Ryan as he caught the ball. "Ryan, throw the ball to me."

Ryan did as Nathan instructed. "How was that, Coach?"

"Very good." Nathan readied his bat again. "Okay, here comes another ball."

Melanie watched for another hour while Nathan had the boys catching and throwing the ball with a fair amount of ease. Every once in a while, Nathan glanced in her direction and smiled. Every time her heart did that crazy little flip-flop. She was having a hard time keeping her thoughts from drifting into that dangerous personal territory that was better forgotten.

"Are you guys ready for a little game?"

Ryan and Andrew jumped up and down. "Yeah."

Stopping, Andrew gazed up at Nathan. "Can our mom play, too?"

Nathan motioned for her to join them. "Come on, Mom. You can get in the game."

Tightness building in her chest, Melanie stepped off the deck. "I'm not very good at this kind of stuff."

"Andrew can help you." Nathan's suggestion was a huge confidence booster for her younger son.

"Yeah, Mom. I can show you how to bat. You're already good at throwing the ball." Andrew picked up the bat and took the stance that Nathan had showed him. "This is how you get ready to hit the ball."

Nathan grinned. "Let's see if you can hit this pitch."

Andrew handed her the bat, and she tried to imitate what her son had done. "Andrew, is this right?"

"That's good, Mom." Andrew turned to Nathan. "Coach Nathan, throw her the ball."

The ball came toward her. She swung and missed. Why was she embarrassing herself? *For her kids.* Everything she did was for her little boys. She wanted them to have a wonderful life. But she didn't want to look at Nathan. He was probably thinking she was a terrible athlete. She'd always hated gym class when she was in school for this very reason.

"That's okay, Mom. You can hit the next one. You get three strikes, you know." Andrew's little voice cheered her.

Taking a deep breath, she took her stance again and looked at Nathan. When he smiled, she forgot to look at the ball until it whizzed by her. She missed again.

Ryan clapped his hands. "Come on, Mom. You can hit it this time."

"Okay." This was her last chance. The ball raced toward her. She swung. She wasn't even sure she'd had her eyes open when she hit the ball, but when she looked up, it was sailing over Nathan's head. Cheering wildly, Ryan and Andrew chased it.

Walking toward her, Nathan smiled. "That was a good hit. You're a quick study. You can be on my team anytime."

Melanie chuckled. "I don't plan on participating in any baseball games. I'll leave that to you and the boys. Watching is more my speed."

"Have you ever been to Ray and Barbara Keller's Memorial Day picnic?"

Melanie shook her head. "We always go to visit Tim's parents over Memorial Day."

"Why don't you ask them to visit you and attend the picnic? Then I can pick you for my team when we play softball."

"Besides not wanting to play softball, we couldn't crash the party."

"You wouldn't be crashing. You'd be my guests."

Melanie wondered whether he was extending this invitation because he was interested in being with her, or whether he was just being polite to a bank customer. She didn't dare ask. Besides it was a moot point. She couldn't go. "I'm sorry. Tim's parents would never change their plans. Their calendar is written in stone, if you know what I mean."

"I understand."

"Mom, do we have to go to Grandma and Grandpa's? Can't we go to the picnic with Coach Nathan?" Ryan wrinkled his nose. "Grandma smells funny."

"That's not a nice thing to say, so don't say it again. It's just her perfume, sweety." Melanie stifled a grin as she looked at Nathan, who also seemed to be holding back laughter.

Nathan picked up the bat and handed it to Ryan. "Okay, it's your turn."

During the next half hour Melanie and Nathan played a three-inning game against Ryan and Andrew. For the first time in her life, she actually enjoyed playing a sport. When the game was over, the boys had won. Their pride in victory filled Melanie's heart with happiness. They needed to feel good about themselves. And the way Nathan encouraged her sons filled her heart with longing and her mind with thoughts that she didn't want to think.

Nathan helped the boys gather the equipment. "We had a good practice, and you guys are ready to get on a team. So I'll head home."

Andrew tugged on Nathan's arm. "You don't have to leave. You can stay for supper. We're having spaghetti, and my mom makes the best."

Nathan glanced over at Melanie, then looked back at

Andrew. "Thanks for inviting me, but I'm sure your mom wasn't planning on having company for supper."

Ryan gazed up at Melanie. "Please say he can eat with us."

"Boys, maybe Mr. Keller already has plans for the evening."

Andrew turned to Nathan. "Do you?"

Nathan chuckled. "No. I don't have plans."

Ryan and Andrew cheered.

"I don't want to impose." Nathan looked at her.

"You're not imposing. If you can stay, we'd like for you to have supper with us."

"Okay. I can always use a home-cooked meal."

The boys cheered again as they walked with Nathan toward the house. Was she inviting Nathan to stay for supper because of her sons or because she wanted to spend more time with him? She wasn't going to tackle that question tonight. She was just going to enjoy the evening and figure out the answer to that question tomorrow.

Chapter Four

A delicious aroma greeted Nathan as he followed Melanie into the house. Going immediately to the stove, she left him standing in the breakfast nook. He wondered whether she'd felt trapped into inviting him to supper.

She looked at Ryan and Andrew, who had come in the back door and dumped their baseball equipment near him in the breakfast nook.

"Hey, guys, where does that stuff go?"

"In the garage," they chorused.

Melanie got a bag of ready-made garlic bread from the freezer. "Okay, then, put your stuff out there. After that, you can wash your hands."

Scrambling to obey their mother, the boys picked up their gear and headed for the door leading to the garage on the other side of the kitchen. Nathan took in the scene, noticing how Ryan and Andrew were eager to please their mother. So far today he hadn't seen a sign of the kids who had squabbled over the video game. Had their fight been an anomaly? Somehow he doubted that, but he had to reserve judgment. Maybe he was projecting too much of his own childhood onto these boys. Still, he couldn't help seeing himself and his brother and their numerous squabbles growing up every time he watched Ryan and Andrew.

Taking in the light wood cabinets and granite countertops of Melanie's spotless kitchen, Nathan wondered about washing his own hands. Why was he feeling like one of the kids who needed instructions? "Where would you like me to wash up?"

Melanie spun around almost as if she'd forgotten that he was there, but she smiled. "Um...the boys can show you."

Before Nathan could respond, Ryan and Andrew raced back into the room. Melanie grabbed Ryan's arm, and both boys stopped and looked wide-eyed at her. "Please show Coach Nathan where he can wash his hands, too."

"Okay, Mom." Ryan turned. "Coach Nathan, come with us."

Nathan followed the twosome through the kitchen to a short hallway. The boys jostled for position as they raced to be the first one to reach the door on their left. Inching out his brother, Ryan opened the door and flipped on the light.

Andrew stopped in the doorway. "Ryan, you should let Coach go first. That's what Mom would say."

Ryan stepped out of the half bath and glared at Andrew. "I was just turning on the light for him."

Nathan fought back a smile. Sibling rivalry was alive and well, after all. He moved past Ryan and into the tiny room. "Thanks."

While Nathan washed his hands, the boys stood in the doorway and stared at him. Many years had passed since he'd had someone watch him wash his hands. That someone had been his mother, who was making sure he'd done a good job. The fact that they were gazing at him so intently told him that these little boys had his every move under scrutiny. He wasn't sure how he felt about that. He'd have to be careful to set a good example. Had his commitment to help these youngsters been more than he'd bargained for?

"Coach, do you think our mom's pretty?" Ryan gazed up at Nathan.

Drying his hands, he took in their wide-eyed expressions, while an avalanche of questions crashed through his mind. Yeah, he thought she was pretty, but did he dare say that to her sons? Why were they asking anyway? Were they trying to be little matchmakers? Would they report his response to her? How could he possibly answer the question without getting himself into all kinds of trouble? Was there any way to avoid answering?

Honesty is the best policy. That's what his parents had taught him. Yeah. He had to be honest no matter the consequences. "Yes, your mom is very pretty."

Andrew peered up at Nathan. "Do you like her?"

Why were they peppering him with these questions— questions he didn't want to answer? If he answered this one, would they have another one waiting for him? He stepped into the hallway. "Of course, I like your mother. She is very nice."

"I knew you would." Ryan grinned as he proceeded to wash his hands.

Nathan wondered about the child's statement. Was his attraction to Melanie, which he'd been trying to tamp down, that apparent, even to her children? He hoped not.

"And you'll really like her spaghetti." Andrew took his turn washing his hands.

"I'm sure I will." Hoping the boys' questions were only innocent curiosity, Nathan studied the photo collages that hung on the walls outside the half bath. They told of happy times. He thought about the conversation he'd had with Melanie about Tim. Nathan could imagine how much her husband's death must have turned her world upside down. Could he be a little part of making it right again, or would he be stepping in where he wasn't needed? Or would his presence build expectations in the minds of these boys? Expectations that he couldn't deliver.

Andrew tapped Nathan on the arm. "Come on, Coach. Let's go."

"Okay. I'm ready for some of your mom's great spaghetti." Nathan joined the boys as they hurried back into the kitchen.

As they came through the door, Melanie looked up from the stove, where she was pouring spaghetti sauce and meatballs into a bowl. "Boys, please set the table. Everything's on the counter."

Ryan rushed forward. "I've got the plates and salad bowls."

Without an argument, Andrew took the flatware and napkins.

Nathan looked at Melanie. "Is there something I can do?"

She smiled, and his heart thumped. He almost forgot to smile in response. Was her smile always going to put his mind on a path it shouldn't take? Maybe his attraction resulted from the power of suggestion—Juliane's suggestion and the speculation prompted by the questions of two little boys.

"Sure. Put this on the table." She held out the bowl containing the spaghetti and meatballs.

"Okay." He carefully took the bowl, making sure not to let their hands touch. Any contact might mess with his mind more than her smile already did. He hurried to the table and set the bowl next to the white teapot centerpiece filled with little blue bell-shaped flowers that matched the color of the woven placemats. Everything was perfect, almost as if she'd expected company for supper. He turned back to her. "Anything else?"

"No. We're ready to eat." She carried a basket containing the garlic bread and a bowl of salad.

Melanie put the bread and salad on the table as the boys sat down. Feeling like an interloper, Nathan took the remaining seat. He was very aware that he was probably sitting in the place where Tim Drake had sat. The thought made Nathan uncomfortable. As he put his napkin on his lap, he observed the two boys and hoped they wouldn't be giving their mother a report on the conversation that had occurred while they had washed their hands.

Melanie looked at him. "Would you say the blessing for us?"

Nathan nodded and bowed his head, trying not to think about Tim Drake or the probability of two little boys divulging information that Nathan preferred not to share. After Nathan said a short prayer, he looked up. When his eyes met Melanie's, his heart did that funny little dance that made it thump against his rib cage.

Nathan quickly turned his attention to Ryan who sat across the table from him. "Are you ready for school to be out for the summer?"

"Yeah, so we can play baseball." Ryan filled his bowl with salad, then passed it to Nathan.

Nathan stared at the bowl. He couldn't eat salad because it could trigger problems related to his Crohn's disease, but he didn't say that. Many people had never heard of the disease, and he didn't want to go into an explanation of his problems. Besides, it wasn't exactly the best topic for a dinner conversation. Could he get by with only saying he didn't eat salads? Had Melanie noticed that he hadn't eaten salads or any raw vegetables when they'd eaten at the club?

Nathan passed the salad to Melanie. "Thanks, but I'm not going to have any."

"Coach Nathan, you should eat salad. Mom says it's good for you." Ryan poured dressing on his salad.

"Your mother is right, but unfortunately raw vegetables don't agree with my digestive system, so I can't eat them."

Andrew took some salad and smothered it with dressing. "I learned about the digestive system in school. That means your stomach and intestines. And your sophigus."

"That's e-sophagus." Ryan gave Andrew a superior look.

Ignoring Ryan's comment, Andrew dug into his spaghetti.

Ryan glanced over at his mother as he took a big helping of spaghetti. "Do you think we can practice baseball while we're at Grandma and Grandpa's?"

Melanie shook her head. "You know your grandmother doesn't like to have her yard trampled."

Ryan frowned. "Didn't Dad ever play baseball in his yard when he was our age?"

"I don't know." Melanie shrugged. "I didn't know your dad when he was a kid. I imagine he practiced at a ball field."

"I'm glad you let us practice in the yard." Andrew smiled at his mother.

"I'm glad we have a big yard so you can practice here, too." Melanie smiled, but her lips appeared to quiver as she quickly looked down at her plate.

Taking a bite of a meatball, Nathan didn't mind that the boys had apparently forgotten about the conversation that they'd had while they washed their hands. Or maybe his worry that they would mention it was unfounded. He was also glad that the new topic was baseball and not his problem with salad. But he wondered whether the talk about Tim and baseball was making Melanie sad. Could he do anything to help? He doubted it. He hated the helpless feeling her sadness evoked. While he pondered the situation, the splendid flavor of the spaghetti tantalized his taste buds.

Nathan looked over at Andrew. "Andrew, you were absolutely right. This is the best spaghetti I've ever tasted."

Sitting up tall, the young boy smiled at his mother. "Mom, you're the bestest cook."

Melanie laughed and the sadness in her dark eyes disappeared. "Thanks, Andrew."

"You're the best mom ever," Ryan said, obviously trying not to be outdone by his younger brother in the compliment department.

Looking at Melanie's pleased expression, Nathan had a delighted feeling. After learning that she had no real family, he sensed that she needed as much encouragement as her boys. Even if it was driven by competition, he was glad to see her boys praising her. Nathan wanted to help, too. "Where did you learn to make such fantastic spaghetti?"

Melanie hunched her shoulders, but Nathan didn't miss the joy that his question brought to her eyes. "From Stella Casalino."

"And who is Stella Casalino?"

Melanie hesitated, almost as if she wasn't sure what to say. She took a deep breath. "You remember my telling you how I grew up in foster care?"

Nathan nodded. "I do."

"Well, when I turned eighteen, I was too old for foster care and on my own."

"You mean they just let you fend for yourself?"

"That's right."

"That's terrible." Nathan frowned.

"I know. Lots of kids like me wind up on the streets or in jail. Fortunately, a friend from one of my high school classes told her parents about me. They invited me to stay with them for the summer before I went to college. They were Christians, and I attended church for the first time. That's where I learned about God's love. And I began to believe that someone really, really cared about me—God and the Millers."

"You mean you'd never been to church in your life before that?"

"Never."

Nathan couldn't mask his incredulity. "I can't imagine. Church has been part of my life since I was born. I grew up going to church and hearing Bible stories."

Melanie glanced at Ryan and Andrew, who were busy eating. "I'm so glad my boys are growing up like you did— knowing about God's love and how He sent His Son Jesus, to die for our sins."

"Me, too." Nathan knew now, more than ever, that he wanted to be a good influence in the lives of these little boys. "So how does this relate to Stella Casalino?"

"Angela Miller is my friend's mom, and Stella was Angela's Italian grandmother. Until she died at the age of ninety-four, she also lived with them and often cooked meals. I took it all in because I'd never been given the chance to cook. She was thrilled that someone was interested and spent hours show- ing me how to make these wonderful Italian dishes. When Tim and I got married, she gave me this little hand-written cookbook with many of her favorite recipes in it."

"So that's that secret to your fabulous spaghetti."

Melanie chuckled. "Poor Tim. When we got married, I served him Italian food until he could barely stand to look at pasta. So we took cooking lessons together and learned to make all kinds of delicious things."

Her amusing reminiscence brightened Nathan's thoughts. He couldn't relate to her loss, but he was happy that every memory of Tim didn't make her sad. Did he dare ask another question about Tim? "Was Tim a good cook?"

"Dad made awesome beef stew," Andrew said.

"I liked his enchiladas best." Ryan again tried to make a

superior statement in a game of one-upmanship with his little brother.

Taking another bite of spaghetti, Nathan wondered whether each conversation would result in the brothers trying to outdo each other.

Ryan set his fork on his plate. "Mom, can we show Coach Nathan Dad's trophies?"

"He might not have time." Melanie's reluctant smile appeared again as she looked at him.

He could see the hesitation in her smile. He wasn't sure what to say. He wished he knew what would put her at ease. What would it take to make that smile genuine again? How did she want him to answer? If he said yes, he had the suspicion that she would feel awkward, but, on the other hand, if he said no, he would disappoint the boys. How could he handle this?

"I have all the time in the world. So it's up to you."

The two boys looked expectantly at Melanie. She sighed. "I suppose that'll be okay."

"All right," the boys chorused.

"Now finish your meal, or you won't be showing Coach Nathan anything."

Nathan wasn't sure, but he suspected that the shine he'd seen in Melanie's eyes was unshed tears. The conversation kept coming back to Tim, and Nathan figured that the poignant reminders of her deceased husband made her emotional. Nathan wished he could take away her sadness, but he had to keep those kinds of thoughts in check. She probably didn't want his comfort.

After they cleaned up the kitchen, they all went to the basement. A pool table dominated the large finished room that took up most of the basement. A wall of shelves held numerous trophies, plaques, books and boxed board games.

Ryan rushed over and plucked a trophy from a lower shelf

and held it up for Nathan to see. "My dad got this one when his high school team won the baseball championship."

Andrew grabbed another one and hoisted it toward Nathan. "He got this one for being MVP on his team."

"Your dad was a good athlete."

"Yeah. That's what Grandpa always says." Ryan replaced the trophy.

Nathan looked at Melanie to see whether she had any reaction to the mention of Tim's father, but a stoic expression masked any response. Nathan still wondered how her former in-laws could possibly dislike her.

After listening to Melanie and the boys talk about Tim, Nathan regretted that he'd been consumed with bank business and had never taken the time to get to know Tim when the family first moved to this town. They could've shared their love for baseball. Nathan tried to rationalize that the Drakes hadn't been in town very long before Tim died, but that thinking didn't eliminate the twinge of guilt that hovered at the edge of his conscience while Ryan and Andrew showed off more of their father's trophies.

When they were done, Andrew followed Melanie up the stairs. "Mom, can we play a game of Sorry with Coach Nathan?"

"Andrew, I think you boys have taken up enough of Coach Nathan's time tonight." Stopping at the top of the stairs, Melanie turned and looked over the top of Andrew's head at Nathan. "I'm sorry they're taking advantage of your kindness."

Again, Nathan wished he knew what Melanie was thinking. He wished he were better at reading the expression in her dark eyes. Did she hope he'd leave, or was she worried that he was feeling put upon? "Honestly, I don't mind."

"See, Mom? I knew he'd like to play a game with us. I'll set up the board." Ryan sprinted to the shelf and grabbed the box containing the game, then raced up the stairs, charging past Melanie on the way.

Shaking her head, Melanie gave Nathan a helpless smile as Andrew chased after his brother. "You are too nice to do this."

"Not so much nice. More like competitive. There's nothing like a good game of Sorry." Following Melanie into the den, Nathan couldn't remember the last time he'd taken the time to play a board game. He realized how much fun the evening had been. He didn't want it to end.

While the boys set up the game on the coffee table in front of him, Nathan sat on the couch and surveyed the den. Framed, family photographs sat on the built-in bookshelves on either side of the fireplace. One large picture of Melanie, Tim, Ryan and Andrew, obviously the work of a professional photographer, hung above the mantel. Nathan knew he was being paranoid, but he could almost feel Tim Drake's eyes staring at him from across the room. They seemed to say, "Stay away from my wife."

Nathan shook the crazy thought from his head. His imagination was working overtime. He had no intentions of getting involved with Melanie. His busy schedule and his Crohn's disease remained obstacles that would keep him from having a good relationship with any woman. Nathan knew his disease wasn't life-threatening, but it was chronic and something he had to live with day in and day out.

While they played the game, Nathan was careful to avoid looking in the direction of that family portrait. He was here for the boys, and that was all. He didn't intend to spend time in Melanie's house other than tonight. He would help her boys on the baseball field. That was where their relationship would begin and end.

When Melanie won the game, she grinned and raised her hands above her head in victory. "That was fun."

Laughing, Nathan enjoyed seeing her expression of triumph. "Yeah. Fun for you because you won. Looks like I'm not the only one who's competitive."

Shaking her head, Melanie smiled shyly. "I've never thought of myself in those terms, but maybe I am."

"We should play another game." Ryan started setting up the board again.

Melanie grabbed Ryan's hand. "Oh, no. You boys have to get ready for bed. We have church in the morning."

"But, Mom." Ryan stuck out his lower lip.

"Coach Nathan, will we see you at church tomorrow?"

"Yes, and your mom's right that you need a good night's rest before then. I'll help you put up the game, and I'll see you tomorrow." Nathan picked up the game pieces and started putting them in the box. He hoped she understood that he was trying to support her quest to get her kids into bed rather than thinking that he wanted to rush off.

"I suppose." Ryan wrinkled his nose but helped Nathan and Andrew put the game away.

When they finished, Melanie ushered the boys toward their rooms. "Tell Coach Nathan thank you, then go get ready for bed. You have to wash up and brush your teeth. After our guest leaves, I'll come in and check on you."

Ryan came over and held out his hand to Nathan. "Thanks, Coach, for helping us with baseball and playing the game with us."

Nathan shook Ryan's hand. "You're welcome. Thanks for inviting me to supper. I had a good time."

Mimicking Ryan, Andrew shook Nathan's hand. "Thank you for teaching me about baseball. Will you come another time and play Sorry with us, so we can beat my mom?"

Nathan glanced at Melanie, then back at Andrew. "Maybe she wants to remain the champ."

"But she has to accept our challenge." Andrew knit his little eyebrows.

Nathan nodded. "She probably does."

"Does that mean you're going to play with us again?"

"Boys, please don't pester Coach Nathan. You don't need him here to play Sorry."

"But, Mom, it's more fun with four."

"That's enough." Melanie pointed toward the hallway. "Say good night, and get going. It's already getting late."

"Good night, Coach," the boys chorused as Melanie waved them out of the room.

As the boys disappeared into the hallway, Melanie turned. Looking uncomfortable, she held a smile in place. "I want to add my thanks. And I'm sorry the boys were such pests tonight."

"You don't have to apologize for them. I like their enthusiasm." Nathan headed toward the front door. "I'd better get going, so you can get them into bed.

"Sometimes they are a handful." Melanie sighed. "There's never a dull moment around here."

"I'm sure that's true. They remind me of my brother and me."

"I didn't know you had a brother. Does he live in town?"

Nathan shook his head. "He lives in New York City."

"Wow! That's far removed from Kellerville. What does he do there?"

"He's an investment banker."

"So he's in banking, too."

"Yeah, but a much different banking atmosphere." Nathan laughed halfheartedly as he opened the door. "He wanted to be a little fish in a big pond, and I wanted to be a big fish in a little pond."

"I'm with you. I'd rather live in a small town. That's why I like Kellerville so much." Melanie switched on the porch light. "Columbus was big enough. I can't imagine living in New York City."

Nathan stepped onto the front porch. "Thanks again for supper."

"I should be the one thanking you for your help."

"That's my job. So no thanks needed."

"But this stuff with the boys was above and beyond your job description." Melanie joined him on the porch as the glass storm door slowly closed behind her.

Nathan chuckled. "I enjoyed it. You and your boys reminded me that I should take a little time out to have some fun. Good night."

"Good night." Standing on the porch, Melanie waved as Nathan made his way to his SUV.

As he backed out of the driveway, she stood silhouetted against the light coming through the front door. He tried not to think of how tempted he was to toss aside the reasons he shouldn't be interested in Melanie Drake. He wasn't sure what he wanted. One minute he was telling himself that he shouldn't have an interest in her, and the next he was wishing he could spend more time with her.

Was Juliane right when she'd said that he needed to have a little more social life? Somehow he doubted that he could let go of his fear of rejection no matter how tempted he was to pursue Melanie. At least not tonight, or even in the near future, maybe never. But could he be her friend—just a friend?

Chapter Five

A lively praise hymn sounded throughout the sanctuary as Melanie sat with Ryan and Andrew in a pew near the front. They'd been asking to see Nathan ever since they had gotten up this morning. Their inquiries did nothing to help her stop thinking about him. Besides, she worried that the boys would bug Nathan when they saw him and make major pests of themselves. She wondered why the boys had attached themselves to Nathan so quick. Hopefully, it wouldn't become a problem.

Next weekend they'd be seeing Tim's parents. Although she had little enthusiasm for the visit, the time with her former in-laws would remind her why she couldn't let an interest in Nathan Keller tempt her. She hoped the boys wouldn't mention Nathan while they were visiting. Tim's parents might jump to the wrong conclusion, and her denial would probably come across as disingenuous because Nathan did spark an attraction—one that she couldn't afford to act upon.

Melanie forced herself to stop thinking about Nathan and Tim's parents. Concentrating on the reason she was in church, she filled her heart with worship for God. She needed to let thoughts of Him fill her mind rather than her worries. She let God's majesty consume her thoughts as she sang the next song.

Before the sermon, the time came for the elementary school children to leave for a special children's church. As Ryan and Andrew exited the pew, Ryan whispered to her. "When will we see Coach Nathan?"

Tamping down her exasperation, Melanie eyed Ryan. "I'm sure you'll get to see him after church."

As Ryan left, he muttered something under his breath. Melanie let him pass without a comment, glad she didn't know what he'd said. The worship service wasn't the place to have a confrontation with one of her sons. Trying to let the incident fade from her thoughts, she bowed her head as the minister started his sermon with a prayer. She prayed for wisdom in dealing with her kids, then settled in to listen to the morning's message.

After the church service ended, Barbara and Ray Keller, who sat in the pew ahead of her, turned to talk to her. While they were conversing, Ryan and Andrew raced up to her. "Boys, please no running in church."

"But, Mom, we wanted to see Coach Nathan." Andrew looked around.

Barbara placed a hand on Melanie's arm. "Is Andrew talking about my nephew?"

Melanie nodded, tension building in her shoulders. "He helped Ryan and Andrew with baseball yesterday, and they've been bugging me ever since to see him again.

"There he is." Ryan rushed out of the pew.

Although Ryan escaped Melanie's grasp, she managed to grab Andrew by the arm before he got away. She looked down at him. "You can't go chasing after your brother."

"But I want to see Coach Nathan, too."

"Melanie, it's okay. Nathan won't mind." Barbara smiled.

Despite her misgivings, Melanie couldn't argue with Barbara. The older woman obviously knew her nephew much better than Melanie did. "All right, but no running and be polite."

"Okay, Mom." Andrew started to run, but after two steps he slowed his pace as he glanced over his shoulder at his mother.

Nodding, Melanie signaled her approval as Andrew leisurely joined his brother, who stood waiting behind Nathan as he talked with another man from the congregation. She breathed a sigh of relief that Ryan hadn't run up to Nathan and interrupted his conversation, but tension once again knotted her shoulders as she watched to see how Nathan would react to their presence. She prayed that he would welcome the attention of her little boys.

Nathan shook hands with the other man, then turned. He immediately noticed Ryan and Andrew. Grinning, Nathan patted each of the boys on the head. Melanie's heart fluttered at the sight of Nathan's kindness toward her sons. His interaction with them said a lot of good things about him.

"See? You had no reason to worry." Barbara's voice made Melanie turn. "I told you Nathan wouldn't mind."

Nodding, Melanie smiled sheepishly. "You're right. I should've known. Nathan was so kind to them yesterday while he taught them about baseball."

"He loves baseball."

"Who loves baseball?" Juliane gave her mother a hug.

"Nathan."

"I should've known. Mention baseball, and Nathan is there."

"Have you seen Elise and Seth?" Barbara asked.

"Yeah, the lovebirds are picking up Olivia from her class. They said they'd meet us at the café."

"Good. Dad and I are going to drive Grandpa and Grandma Keller over there. See you in a few minutes."

"Okay." As her parents left, Juliane glanced at Melanie and

motioned toward Nathan. "I see your boys with Nathan. Did he get them signed up for baseball?"

"How'd you know about that?" Melanie knit her eyebrows.

Juliane shrugged. "Nathan mentioned it one time when we were talking."

"Well, I hope he won't regret it." Melanie glanced at her boys. "They seem to have adopted him. He's their new hero."

Juliane laughed. "Don't tell that to Nathan. It'll give him a big head."

"I don't think anyone will have to tell him. He'll probably figure it out for himself. I suppose I should go rescue him from my kids." Melanie turned to leave.

Juliane touched Melanie's arm. "Hey, why don't you and the boys join us for lunch? We're celebrating my grandmother's eightieth birthday over at the café."

Melanie shook her head. "It's your family's celebration. We'd be crashing your party."

"No. Grandma would love to have some more little ones around. She always says the great grandkids keep her young. Having youngsters around always brightens her day. The more, the merrier."

"You and Lukas should have some kids. That would really brighten her day."

Juliane blushed. "Give us time. We haven't even been married a year."

"I know, but your anniversary's coming up soon. I sure wish I could've been at your wedding, but I'm coming to Elise's. No in-laws to visit this time. We're going up there this coming weekend for Memorial Day."

"Oh, that means you won't get to come to the party at my folks' house."

"I know. Nathan already mentioned that."

Juliane raised her eyebrows. "He did, huh?"

Wishing she'd thought before speaking, Melanie wanted to kick herself. Why had she mentioned this to Juliane? "Don't get any ideas."

"Who's getting ideas?"

"I saw that look."

"Your imagination…or maybe something really is going on between you two." Juliane grinned, then glanced over Melanie's shoulder. "Here come the boys."

Melanie didn't want to turn around. She pretty much guessed that "the boys" included Nathan. Why was she feeling this way? This was so stupid. She didn't need to be afraid of Nathan Keller or her reaction to him. She should be glad her sons had another good male role model in their lives.

"Mom, see what Coach Nathan gave us." Ryan handed Melanie a stack of papers held together by a clip.

"What's this?"

Andrew wiggled his way past Ryan. "Ways we can practice."

Melanie looked up at Nathan. "Are these instructions for me?"

"If you want to look at it that way. Yes." Nathan grinned. "The packet contains suggestions for games you can play with the boys that'll help them with some of their baseball skills."

"Thanks. I think." Melanie folded the papers and stuck them in the side pocket of the cover on her Bible. "We'll look at these when we get home."

Clutching the back of the pew, Juliane leaned toward Melanie. "You're all going to join us for lunch, right?"

Melanie knew Juliane had set the trap with her question. There was no backing out now that the boys had heard the invitation. Melanie manufactured a smile. "Sure."

Nathan eyed her. "Would you like a ride to the café?"

Melanie's mind buzzed around Nathan's invitation. She was probably reading way more into it than she should. What would Juliane say about it, since she'd already inferred that something was going on between Melanie and Nathan?

"Mom, can we?" Ryan asked before Melanie could gather her thoughts and formulate an answer.

Her thoughts moved through her brain in slow motion as she looked up at Nathan, then at Ryan and Andrew. Everyone was waiting for her answer. "Thanks, but it's such a nice day, I think we'll walk. The café is only a few blocks from the church, so it'll be a lovely stroll, besides being good exercise."

"That's an excellent idea. I'll walk with you." Nathan ruffled the boys' hair. "Are you fellas up for some good exercise?"

"Yeah," they chorused.

"Great idea, Melanie. We can all walk over together. No sense in everyone driving a car." Juliane glanced around the nearly empty sanctuary. "Wait for me while I find Lukas. I think he's talking with Pastor Tom."

Holding out one hand, Nathan indicated that Melanie should go ahead of him up the aisle. "We'll meet you out front."

Trying not to think about how this walk meant spending more time with Nathan, she proceeded to the door that led to the foyer. She should've taken the two-minute ride. Now she was in for a ten-minute walk. Why was she letting this whole thing make her crazy? Blame it on Juliane. She'd started it with her suggestion that Melanie and Nathan had an interest in each other that went beyond their business dealings and youth baseball.

As Nathan fell into step beside her, Ryan and Andrew scrambled to beat each other to the doors. She didn't want to scold her boys again. Melanie cringed, wondering what

Nathan must think. Could they ever remember just to walk? Was it possible that their participation in baseball would eat up some of their energy?

"Hey, thanks again for the great spaghetti last night." Nathan opened the door for her. "I'm glad you're joining our celebration today. Grandma will love your boys."

"I feel kind of funny about this."

"You mean about attending this party?"

Melanie nodded. "I hardly know your grandmother. I met her one time at church. And besides, we don't have a gift. Not even a card."

"Believe me. Grandma isn't going to care. They'll be so much stuff that she won't know who brought her what." Lukas and Juliane came out the front doors, and Nathan waved them over. "Juliane, tell Melanie that she shouldn't be worried about not having a gift."

"Nathan's right. This isn't about gifts. Grandma couldn't care less about that. This is about being together with family and friends to share in a celebration of this milestone in her life."

Melanie hunched her shoulders. "I hope you're right."

"I am." Chuckling, Nathan motioned toward Ryan and Andrew, who were sprinting ahead. "I can't believe kids still play that game."

"What game?"

"Not stepping on the cracks in the sidewalk."

"I think they must've learned that at school. I never played that game when I was kid."

"You didn't?" Disbelief was written all over Nathan's face.

"As you know, I didn't have the typical childhood."

Regret replaced the disbelief in Nathan's expression. "I keep sticking my foot in my mouth. I should've remembered that."

"That's okay. As I said before, I'm just glad my boys won't go through what I did. Even though they've lost their father, they have men like Lukas and you to give them some guidance."

Nathan gave her a sideways glance. "Any time you need help with anything, please let me know."

"Thanks." Melanie nodded, hoping that no one, especially Nathan, considered her and her children a nuisance.

Questions crowded her mind as they walked past the stores on Main Street. Was his willingness to help part of that Christian teaching about helping widows and orphans, or did he have a more personal interest? Would asking him to help her on occasion set her up to like him too much? She was afraid to answer these questions. Giving herself a mental shake, she knew she had to quit thinking about it. She couldn't let herself become emotionally involved with any man right now.

When they entered the café, owned by one of the Keller clan, the place already hummed with activity. Putting her arms around her sons' shoulders, Melanie corralled them as they followed Nathan into a large private room located on one side of the restaurant. A two-tiered cake sat on a table in one corner. Another table contained a pile of gaily wrapped packages while festive balloons and streamers decorated each table.

"There's Grandpa and Grandma Keller." Juliane pointed to the table near the window. "Grandma looks so jovial in her birthday hat. She loves being the birthday girl."

"I can't believe she's wearing it." Nathan chuckled. "It's supposed to be for decoration, but you know Grandma. She doesn't mind playing the clown—anything for a laugh."

Juliane slipped her arm through Lukas's. "Let's go say hi to the birthday girl. She's eating up the attention."

Looking in that direction, Melanie recognized the older couple. She hung back as the group made its way across the room to greet Addie Keller. After Juliane, Lukas and Nathan wished their grandmother a happy birthday, Juliane gave Melanie a nudge forward, then introduced her and the boys to the older woman.

"I'm so happy that you came to celebrate with me. I remember you, dear. I've been praying for you and your sweet boys every day since you lost your husband." Patting Melanie's hand, the older woman pulled her close and whispered, "My grandson Nathan could use a wife. You'd be a good one for him. Just keep that in mind. It'll be our little secret, okay?"

Melanie nodded not knowing how else to respond. She wondered whether anyone noticed that she was blushing as heat rose in her cheeks. Hopefully, no one had heard Addie's comment. "Thank you for your prayers."

Addie looked at Ryan and Andrew. "How do you boys like my hat? Olivia thought I should wear it. What do you think?"

Nodding, Andrew shrugged. "It's a good birthday hat, but Nathan thought wearing the hat was your idea. He said you liked playing a clown."

Her stomach sinking, Melanie stared at the floor and hoped when she looked up that Nathan wouldn't be angry. Why did her boys have to embarrass her, even when they weren't being bad? When she finally had the nerve to glance Nathan's way, he was grinning.

Nathan tapped Andrew on the top of his head. "Are you trying to get me into trouble?"

"No, Coach Nathan." Andrew looked puzzled.

Nathan laughed, and Addie leaned over and gave Andrew a hug. "I guess my grandson Nathan knows his grandmother very well."

"I do."

"You boys can go pick a birthday hat, too." Addie pointed toward a table where several youngsters were sitting, including

Olivia, Seth's little three-and-a-half-year-old daughter. "You can get one right over there."

Andrew looked up at Melanie. "Can we?"

Melanie glanced at Juliane, who nodded. "Okay, but behave yourselves."

Nathan chuckled as Andrew and Ryan joined the other children. "Looks like the kids' table."

"It sure does." Juliane laughed. "Remember when we were kids how we always sat at the kids' table at every event?"

"Yeah. I'm so glad I'm a grown-up. No more kids' table."

Her embarrassment subsiding, Melanie took in the good-natured kidding about the birthday hats and talk of growing up as part of the Keller clan. She didn't know how to relate. What would it be like to have a big, boisterous and loving family? She'd had a small taste of it in the few months that she'd lived with the Millers, but she hadn't been there long enough to make that feeling real because she had gone to college in the fall. Even though they had stayed in touch, she'd still felt like an outsider—an attitude of her own making. Then she'd married Tim. He had been the love of her life, but his family hadn't been very loud, boisterous or loving. And she'd been an outsider there as well.

Throughout the rest of the celebratory lunch, everything about Nathan and his family was pulling her in, making her want to be a part. But she didn't want to be drawn in only to be disappointed, as she'd been too many times in her life.

Nothing related to family ever lasted for her. Her parents had abandoned her, each in their own selfish way. She'd been shuffled from foster home to foster home. She'd feared getting too close to anyone, even the Millers who had taken her in and loved her. Losing Tim counted as one more disillusionment in her experience with family. Sometimes she felt that getting close with anyone only led to heartache.

But she couldn't let that attitude color her relationship with

Ryan and Andrew. Her boys were the only family she had left. Her entire existence was built around protecting them and keeping what was left of her family together. She wouldn't let anything separate them.

Ever.

Ryan buckled his seatbelt. "Mom, we can't be late for our first practice."

"You won't be late. We'll swing by the Dairy Barn and pick up some carryout for our supper." Wishing she'd had time to change clothes after work before rushing to pick up her kids, Melanie turned onto the main highway and headed toward the Dairy Barn. People were going to think that her only clothes were the scrubs she wore to work, but she shouldn't be worried about the clothes she was wearing. Doing the best for her sons was the most important thing. "We can eat on our way to the ballpark."

By the time they arrived at the park, the sun sat low in the cloudless sky even though there were several hours of daylight remaining. On the drive to the park, the boys had finished their burgers and fries and were eager to play baseball. As soon as Melanie pulled to a stop in the parking lot, they grabbed their ball caps and gloves and scrambled out of the car.

Children's squeals and laughter greeted Melanie as she slowly got out of her car. Nearby, little ones played on a swing set and jungle gym. The smell of the ball fields' newly mowed grass filled the air. Other parents already packed the bleachers while their youngsters milled in the infield of the ball diamond with the adult volunteers who had organized youth baseball. Did she know any of these parents?

Melanie suddenly realized how isolated she'd become since Tim's death. Except for her grief support group, she'd closed herself off from social events because it hurt too much to go places alone. She hated being a single in the world of couples. Church and work were her only activities outside of the home. She'd failed to nurture her friendship with Juliane. Melanie knew she had to change that.

As she settled on one end of the bleachers by herself, Seth Finley, Elise Keller's fiancé and the director of Kellerville's recreation center, blew a whistle. Ryan and Andrew joined a large group of boys and girls who gathered around Seth as he stood in the pitcher's mound in the middle of the baseball diamond.

Even though the children surrounding Seth listened quietly, Melanie couldn't hear what he was saying. Not that it mattered because she was more concerned that Nathan wasn't here. Strangely enough, the boys hadn't asked about him. Even though she'd made a concerted effort not to think about him, Nathan had been on Melanie's mind ever since his grandmother's birthday and the trip to see the Drakes when her boys had told her how Nathan had said she was pretty. Melanie kept telling herself that Nathan had been trapped into his answers by her sons' questions, but knowing what he'd said made it harder for her to quit thinking about him.

Melanie had expected to see him as soon as they'd arrived at the park. She didn't want to admit being disappointed that he wasn't here. He was one of the coaches. Wasn't he supposed to be here?

Studying the clipboards in their hands, several men and women began calling out the names of the children assigned to different teams. Melanie listened for Ryan and Andrew's names. When she heard Ryan's name, he sprinted toward third base, where a balding middle-aged man stood. She figured that he must be the coach for Ryan's team. A hint of disappointment flitted through her mind because she'd wanted Nathan to be their coach.

Melanie waited to hear them call Andrew's name. After one

of the men called Andrew's name, he also joined the group at third base. While she wondered whether this meant the boys would be on the same team, Nathan seemed to appear out of nowhere. Carrying a large box, he approached the group of children gathered along the third-base line.

Melanie's heart skipped a beat when she saw him. His blue T-shirt, with Kellerville National Bank written across the front in white letters, hugged his muscular torso. He set the box on the ground, then opened it and started handing out shirts to the kids. She realized how much she'd been waiting to see him. Going to Tim's parents had done nothing to blunt the idea of a relationship with Nathan, even though she'd continually told herself that such a relationship wouldn't be prudent. She kept remembering what Addie Keller had whispered at the birthday party. Melanie didn't want to have these feelings, but she couldn't get rid of them. Was she unwise for entertaining the notion?

"Hi, Melanie."

The sound of the female voice took Melanie's attention away from the practice and Nathan. "Juliane, what are you doing here?"

"Lukas is coaching this year." Juliane climbed into the bleachers and sat next to Melanie. "Nathan said he'd pick us up, but he got stuck at the bank, so we're a little late."

"Is Elise here, too?" Melanie glanced around. "I know Seth is in charge of the youth baseball program."

Juliane nodded her head in the direction of the swings. "Yeah, she rode with us, but she took Olivia over there to play."

"It looks like Ryan and Andrew are on Nathan's team. I'm glad." Melanie took in the goings-on that consisted of many of the things that Nathan had shown the boys when he'd come to her house a couple of weeks ago.

Smiling, Juliane raised her eyebrows. "I thought that would make you happy."

"It does because they know him and feel comfortable around him." Melanie watched her boys with a sense of pride as they worked on throwing and catching with the other kids. She and the boys had used the packet of games that Nathan had given them. She could tell that the extra practice was paying off.

"I thought it might make you happy for a different reason."

Pressing her lips together, Melanie wished Juliane wouldn't speculate. Maybe ignoring her hints was the best recourse. "I just hope the two boys get along. Maybe being teammates will make them want to cooperate rather than argue." Melanie shook her head. "Sometimes, they drive me crazy with their quarreling."

Juliane chuckled. "Elise and I used to fight all the time while we were growing up. Now we're best friends."

"So there's hope for my boys?"

"Yeah. How was your trip to see Tim's parents?"

"Okay." Melanie didn't want to talk about the uncomfortable weekend they'd spent with the Drakes. She'd survived the visit, and, thankfully, Ryan and Andrew had been well behaved. The Drakes probably intimidated their only grandchildren into good behavior with their stern demeanor. Melanie wished that Tim's parents were more like Nathan's grandparents. But she could never imagine Georgia Drake wearing a birthday hat as Addie Keller had done or Harlan Drake singing karaoke with Nathan's uncle Ray. Melanie wanted to be part of a big, happy family like the Kellers, but she cautioned herself not to hope for things she couldn't have. "I wish we could've been at your folks' picnic."

"Me, too." Juliane eyed Melanie. "Maybe next year?"

"That's highly unlikely. I can dream, but we'll probably go

to see Tim's parents again. They expect it." Melanie wished she had the nerve to suggest that they come to Kellerville for the holiday, but she knew she'd never make the request. "How are Elise's wedding plans progressing?"

"Everything's under control, even though the bride is driving me crazy. She's a bundle of nerves." Juliane laughed. "She was that way for my wedding, too, even when she wasn't the bride. I guess wedding preparations, no matter whose they are, make her nervous."

"I never had time to be nervous about wedding preparations. Tim and I eloped."

"How romantic!"

Melanie shrugged. "Maybe, but it didn't go over well with his parents. That's why I try not to disrupt their plans these days. I want to stay on their good side."

"I'm so glad you get to come to Elise's wedding." Juliane eyed Melanie. "You know that Nathan's in the wedding party."

"That's nice." Melanie didn't like the turn this conversation was taking. She had a feeling Juliane was hinting at something again.

"I overheard what Grandma Keller said to you at her birthday." Juliane grinned. "I think she's right."

Melanie sighed, wondering whether Nathan had heard, too. Her insides curdled at the thought. "I think you and your grandma are both wishful thinkers. Nathan isn't interested in me romantically any more than I'm interested in him. Let's just leave it at that, okay?"

"Sure."

"Thanks." Somehow Juliane's quick agreement and her own half truth about her feelings for Nathan didn't ease Melanie's mind. Something told her that Juliane wasn't going to let the issue go. She would find a way to bring it up again at the most convenient—or maybe inconvenient—time.

"I have a great thought." Juliane snapped her fingers. "My family is planning a big picnic out at the lake next Saturday. Nathan and his dad are putting their boat in the water for the summer. You and the boys have to come."

Melanie wanted to say yes, but would she be crashing another Keller family party? Would another gathering of the Keller clan leave her yearning to be a part of this family? But hadn't she just told herself that she needed to cultivate her friendship with Juliane? "That sounds like it would be fun. Do I need to bring anything?"

"Probably not, but I'll let you know. There's usually so much food that we have tons of leftovers."

Melanie glanced toward the area of the ball field where Nathan and his assistant were still conducting drills. "I can hardly wait to see the kids play a real game."

"I know. Every year our store has sponsored a team, and we come out and cheer for them. We always have a fun time."

"I see Lukas is coaching the team sponsored by his company. So who are you going to cheer for this year—your store team or Lukas's team?"

"Definitely Lukas's team."

Melanie gave Juliane a sideways glance. "So I guess that means we'll be cheering against one another when our teams play each other."

"Yeah, that's the way it works."

Melanie noticed that Nathan had his kids seated on the ground as he stood in front of them. "Nathan's such a good teacher. He was super with my boys when he was working with them a couple of weeks ago at the house."

Juliane looked at Melanie with surprise. "Nathan was over at your house?"

Melanie's stomach sank. Without thinking, she'd said too much. Now Juliane would suspect more than ever that something was happening between her and Nathan. No sense in trying to disguise the truth. "Yeah, he came over one Saturday afternoon and showed them some basics."

"And you're trying to convince me that nothing's going on between you two?"

"That's right. He was helping Ryan and Andrew. It starts and stops there."

"Okay." Standing, Juliane waved to Lukas, who was gathering his team equipment. "Looks like they're about done."

"You're right." Melanie stepped off the bleachers.

Juliane looked toward the playground, then back at Melanie. "Elise is still pushing Olivia on the swings. Lukas, Seth, Nathan. We're all going to the Dairy Barn for ice cream. You want to join us?"

"Yeah, Mom. Please. Let's go with them."

Melanie whirled around at the sound of Andrew's voice. "Don't you think you've had enough Dairy Barn for one day?"

Ryan came up behind Andrew. "But we didn't have ice cream."

Melanie stared at her sons whose eager expressions made any thought of telling them they couldn't go difficult. What would be the harm? Just as she was about to give an affirmative answer, she looked up. Nathan stood there. Her stomach churned. Would going add to her confusing thoughts about him? She might as well get used to having him around. She couldn't avoid his presence as long as he was coaching the boys' baseball team. Besides, Juliane was the one who kept putting crazy thoughts in her head. Maybe it would help for the other woman to see for herself that there was nothing going on between them.

Melanie nodded. "Sure. I think that's a good idea. I'd love some ice cream."

The whoops and hollers of joy from Ryan and Andrew that followed her answer did nothing to soothe her nerves. But she was going to be brave and step out and take hold of her life. She deserved to have some fun, and if that included Nathan, she would tackle that, too.

Chapter Six

The parking lot of the Dairy Barn overflowed with the cars of the folks who had stopped for a snack after baseball practice. Nathan pulled his SUV into what looked like the last parking place. "I hope we won't have any trouble finding a table."

Juliane pointed toward one of the picnic tables that sat under the maple trees lining one side of the restaurant. "It looks like Seth saved a table for us."

Nathan was disappointed not to see Melanie and her boys sitting there, too. They said they were coming, so he hoped they hadn't changed their minds. He tried to tell himself that he didn't care, but he knew he was kidding himself. He'd tried to stop thinking about her, but instead, he found himself thinking about her more. As Nathan, Lukas and Juliane got out of the SUV, Seth waved them over to the table.

With thoughts of Melanie flooding his head, Nathan settled on the bench in between Seth and Juliane. "So how'd you guys think our first practice went?"

"I'm glad to get the younger kids started with their practice, and I thought everything went very well. What do you think?" Seth glanced back and forth between Nathan and Lukas.

"Since this is my first experience with coaching youth base-ball, I didn't know what to expect, but I'm glad my favorite cheerleader was there." Lukas put his arm around Juliane's shoulders and pulled her close.

"I definitely like being your best fan." She laughed, snuggling against him.

"What kind of ice cream cone should I get for my greatest fan?" Lukas asked.

"Chocolate and vanilla swirl."

"Nathan?"

"You're going to spring for mine, too?"

"Sure. I'm feeling generous tonight."

Nathan chuckled. "I'll have the same as Juliane."

"Okay. I'll be back in no time." Lukas hopped up from the bench and gave Juliane a peck on the cheek before he trotted off to place the order.

Taking in the scene, Nathan couldn't help being envious of his cousin. Could he ever expect to find happiness like Juliane and Lukas? He'd put any thoughts of a romantic relationship out of his mind since his breakup with Andrea, but Melanie had awakened the part of his heart that he thought he'd shut down forever. What was he going to do about it?

"What do you think, Nathan?" Seth's question shook Nathan from his thoughts.

Nathan didn't want to admit he hadn't been listening, so he took a chance and hoped they were still talking about how practice went. "I've got a group of really enthusiastic kids. This ought to be a terrific season for the bank's team. I've got some great plans for next week's practices."

"You definitely have two very excited boys on your team," Seth said.

Glad that he'd guessed correctly on the topic of the conversation, Nathan let Seth's statement soak in and wondered whether he was talking about Ryan and Andrew. "Who?"

"Ryan and Andrew Drake."

Nathan was pleased that Melanie's boys were glad to be on

his team, but he didn't remember seeing Melanie and her kids talking to Seth at practice. "When did you talk to them?"

"A few minutes ago. They are thrilled about playing baseball and being on your team." Seth nodded toward the building. "They're inside with Melanie, Elise and Olivia getting their ice cream."

They were here after all. Nathan's mind buzzed with the thought. He glanced over at the restaurant doors as Melanie and Elise walked outside. Ryan, Andrew and Olivia followed close behind, ice cream cones in hand, as they approached the table. Nathan's stomach somersaulted. He'd just seen Melanie at the ballpark. Why was he so nervous now?

Trying to lick her ice cream cone, Olivia skipped beside the boys. Without warning, the swirl of vanilla ice cream on top of her cone fell off and plopped onto the ground. Stopping, Olivia looked down and started to cry. Seth jumped up and jogged toward the group, but before he got there, Ryan and Andrew tried to comfort the little girl. After Seth picked up Olivia, an animated discussion took place, and the whole group went back into the restaurant. Nathan saw this as a chance to gather his wits before Melanie returned.

"Ryan and Andrew are such sweet boys for trying to make Olivia feel better. Their actions say a lot of good things about the way Melanie is raising them." Juliane looked at Nathan as if she expected him to say something. "So have you been helping out with them like you planned?"

"I got them signed up for baseball. That's about it."

"I still think you should ask Melanie out."

Nathan glared at Juliane. "If I decide to do that, I'll do it without your prompting."

"Oh, so you're considering it?"

Shaking his head, Nathan laughed halfheartedly. "Don't put words in my mouth."

"I thought you put those words in your own mouth."

Nathan narrowed his gaze as he stared at Juliane. "Did someone appoint you the town matchmaker? You're always trying to push people together. First, Seth and Elise—"

"Yeah, and look how well that worked out. I'm doing a pretty good job." Juliane's face beamed. "And you could be next."

Lukas returned with their ice cream and saved Nathan from Juliane's badgering. They ate their cones in silence until the others returned. This time Olivia walked cautiously as she protected her new cone. With Seth's help, she got situated at the table.

While everyone enjoyed the warm evening and the ice cream, Nathan thought about next weekend. His parents were back from their latest trip, and his dad was planning a picnic as he put his boat in the water up at the lake. Nathan was tempted to ask Melanie and her boys to come, but something he couldn't pinpoint kept him from issuing the invitation. Did his reticence still have something to do with Andrea's rejection? He wasn't sure, but he knew he couldn't bring himself to take a chance and invite Melanie.

He tried to tell himself that inviting Melanie wasn't like having a date with her. This would be just a family outing. But neither this line of thinking nor Juliane's pesky comments running through his brain could goad him into asking.

Conversation continued to swirl around Nathan as his thoughts lingered on Melanie. She laughed at something Lukas said. Her joy touched Nathan's heart. He wanted her to be happy, not the woman with tears welling in her eyes that he'd seen the other night at dinner. Did he fit into that picture? If only he were brave enough to find out.

"Ryan, who's that cute little brown-haired girl you were hanging out with at practice tonight?" Lukas's question caught Nathan's attention.

"I wasn't hanging out with no girl." Wrinkling his nose,

Ryan vehemently shook his head. "I don't like girls, 'cept maybe little girls like Olivia. They're okay. That girl was talking to me. I wasn't talking to her. She's on my team and was in my class at school. And Mom says I have to be polite to everyone, even if I don't like it."

"We're too young to hang out with girls." Andrew sat up tall in his seat. "We need to be old like Coach Nathan to like girls. He likes my mom and thinks she's pretty."

While a collective chuckle rose from the adults around the table, except Melanie and him, Nathan wondered whether his face was as red as hers. He quickly dropped his gaze, wishing he could somehow evaporate into thin air. How was he going to explain Andrew's comment without embarrassing Melanie or himself?

Nathan had forgotten how Ryan and Andrew had quizzed him concerning their mother. At the time, he had been worried that they'd bring it up at dinner during the evening, but when they didn't, the episode had completely slipped his mind. He'd been so relieved that they hadn't said anything then. Now he wished they had. That way maybe no one but the four of them would have known, or at least, Melanie would have already known what had transpired.

Now his matchmaking cousin and two of his best buddies knew, and they would tease him unmercifully. He didn't want to be in for a lot of kidding at Melanie's expense. Was there any way to send this conversation in another direction?

Lukas put an arm around Andrew's shoulders. "So, Andrew, tell me how you know this about Coach Nathan here."

"He told us when he ate dinner at our house."

A look passed between Juliane and Melanie before Juliane focused her gaze on Nathan. "You never told me that you had dinner at Melanie's house."

"I didn't know I had to report my activities to you." Standing, Nathan looked at the two boys. "Ryan and Andrew, I believe Olivia would love to play on the slide."

"Yeah, I wanna slide." Olivia clapped her hands.

Nathan glanced at Seth. "Okay if they take her over there?"

"Sure." Seth lifted Olivia out of her seat and set her down on the ground, then gazed at Ryan and Andrew. "Be sure to keep a good eye on her, okay, guys?"

"We will," the boys chorused as they each took one of Olivia's hands and scampered to the nearby playground.

As the kids left, Lukas chuckled and studied Nathan. "Trying to get rid of the witnesses?"

Shaking his head, Nathan resumed his seat. "Quit joking. I think you're embarrassing Melanie. If you want to pick on me that's fine, but do it some other time."

Lukas held up his hands. "Hey, I'm sorry. I wasn't trying to embarrass anyone. I thought Andrew was cute saying you had to be as old as you to like girls."

Rubbing his fingers across his forehead, Nathan couldn't help but laugh. "Okay, I have to admit that was funny."

Nathan glanced over at Melanie, and she laughed as if they were sharing their own private joke. He kind of liked the feeling. Despite, the awkward moment, she seemed to be taking it all in stride. "Thanks for trying to rescue me from the fallout over my son's assessment of romance, but maybe I should've been the one trying to rescue you. When we were on our trip to see their grandparents, they told me about their conversation with you."

"They did?"

"Yeah, and I could see how they put you on the spot." Melanie turned to the others at the table. "My little guys cornered Nathan and asked him if he liked me and thought I was pretty. What was he supposed to say?"

The truth. The phrase zipping through his mind hit the

target like a well-thrown baseball. Yeah. He might as well step up and take responsibility for what he'd said. "Andrew was stating the facts. That's my story, and I'm sticking to it."

Nathan's response brought a collective chuckle to the table.

Melanie glanced to where Ryan and Andrew were playing with Olivia, then back at everyone seated at the picnic table. "I love my boys, but sometimes they can try a person's patience."

"Well, I think you're doing a terrific job with them." Juliane patted Melanie's arm.

Nathan wanted to echo Juliane's sentiments, but he'd already said enough tonight. He was better off to remain silent. He'd managed to get both Ryan and Andrew on his team. He'd kept telling himself his main concern was helping them, but deep in his heart, he knew having them on his team meant seeing more of Melanie. She'd had the courage to tell the group about the incident with her boys and him. He liked that she could laugh at her sons and herself.

He was tempted to throw away his fears and ask her for a date, but he couldn't brush away the same old concerns about getting involved with Melanie. He was constantly busy at the bank, and his Crohn's disease hadn't miraculously been cured. Still, those two obstacles hadn't managed to crush the little seed of interest that had sprung up in his heart since the night he'd eaten her spaghetti and played games with her and her boys. He'd had a taste of what it would be like to have a family of his own, and he couldn't deny that he liked it.

Melanie alternately dreaded and looked forward to the picnic at the lake. When Juliane had insisted on giving Melanie and her boys a ride, she suspected that Juliane was afraid Melanie wouldn't show up, left to drive to the lake on her own. As they turned onto the road that led to the lake, Melanie realized that everything about today made her a little nervous, especially an inevitable conversation with Nathan's parents.

Lukas parked his car near one of the many picnic areas surrounding the lake. The glassy water glistened in the sun beaming from a cloudless sky. Wanting to have an enjoyable day, Melanie hoped to continue the renewal of her friendship with Juliane. But Nathan would be here, too, and Melanie wasn't quite sure what to expect from him. Despite the jovial way he'd taken Andrew's revelations the night of the first baseball practice, Nathan had left immediately after subsequent practices, not joining the group at the Dairy Barn.

Melanie wondered whether he was trying to avoid her and her boys. Her son had embarrassed Nathan, and he was obviously not taking a chance that it would happen again. He was polite and friendly to them at church and at the baseball practices, but she sensed that he was making less effort to be with them. How was he going to act today, and how was she going to handle it?

"Ryan and Andrew, are you ready for a fun day?" Juliane asked, helping Lukas lift a big blue and white cooler from the trunk of their car.

"Yeah. I want to take a ride in the speedboat." Ryan hoisted his backpack over his shoulders. "When do we get to do that?"

"Looks like we're the first ones here, so we'll have to wait until Nathan and his dad get here with the boat." Lukas set the cooler next to one of several picnic tables situated near the water, not too far from the boat ramp.

"Speaking of Nathan and Uncle John, here they are." Juliane nodded toward the road that led to the boat ramp, then glanced at Ryan. "Even though they're going to put the boat in the water now, I think they're not planning to actually take it out until after we eat."

"Do you boys want to go with me and watch them put the boat in?" Lukas asked.

Andrew dumped his backpack on the picnic table. "Yeah. Cool."

"Mom, is that okay?" Ryan set his backpack next to Andrew's.

Surprised that Ryan asked permission, Melanie nodded. "Do what Lukas says, and don't get in the way."

Melanie watched them jog away with Lukas, then turned to Juliane. "Is there something I can help you do?"

"Sure, you can help put these on the tables." Juliane held up some green-and-white-checkered plastic tablecloths. "After that, there isn't much we can do until the others get here."

"Okay." Melanie kept casting glances in the direction of the boat ramp while she helped Juliane. She wanted to make sure the boys were doing okay. But each time she looked she also saw Nathan, and her heart skipped a beat.

"Do you water ski?" Juliane secured the last tablecloth.

"I haven't been on water skis since Tim and I were dating. One of his friends had a ski boat. I have no idea whether I can still do it."

"You'll have to give it a try."

"Maybe." The thought of water-skiing didn't exactly thrill Melanie, especially if she had to make her first attempt in years while Nathan was watching. Another silly thought. Why would he care? And why was she worried about it?

"I bet Ryan and Andrew would like to give it a try."

"Aren't they a little young?" Melanie could just hear Georgia Drake, if she learned that her grandsons were trying to water ski.

"Not really. Several of my teenage cousins are great skiers, and they started when they were the same age as your boys. Nathan started at their age, too."

"We'll see."

"You want to join the guys over at the boat ramp?"

Melanie shrugged. "You can go if you want. I'll stay here and wait for the others to arrive. If I go, my boys might think I'm hovering."

"Is that it, or are you avoiding Nathan? Or maybe you're keeping an eye on him."

"None of the above." Melanie narrowed her gaze. "What makes you ask that?"

"You keep looking over there."

Melanie laughed halfheartedly. "Did it ever occur to you that I'm keeping an eye on my children?"

"Yes, but Nathan's over there, too."

"I know you seem determined to shove us together, but I think you're making a mistake."

"Am I? I can't help thinking about how he stood up for you the other night. I've never seen him so protective."

"I think he was trying to cover his embarrassment. You have to admit that it was a rather awkward situation the way Andrew told everyone what Nathan had said. I know you guys mean well, but I think Nathan and I need to work this thing out on our own." Melanie placed one hand over her heart. "I'm just not sure about dating again. Please let Nathan and me be friends, and we'll see if something else develops, okay?"

Nodding, Juliane gave Melanie a hug. Before Juliane could say anything else, Seth and Elise arrived with Olivia, who immediately begged to join Ryan and Andrew as they watched the boat coming off the trailer. After Seth and Elise put their cooler next to the one Juliane and Lukas had brought, Seth trotted away with Olivia on his shoulders to see the boat.

Elise hugged Juliane and Melanie. "What a perfect day for a picnic!"

Juliane nodded. "Are Mom and Dad on their way?"

"Yeah, I talked to Mom just as they were leaving. They

had to stop by and pick up Aunt Ginny, since Uncle John and Nathan drove the boat up."

Minutes later Ray and Barbara Keller arrived along with Ginny Keller. As they approached, Juliane turned to Melanie. "Have you ever met Nathan's parents?"

"Not really." Although Melanie had seen John and Ginny Keller numerous times at church, she'd never officially met them. Of course, John Keller was the president of the bank, and Ginny Keller was a dean at the local college. They were important people in Kellerville, and they made her nervous, even more nervous than Nathan had made her the day of their first meeting at the bank.

Juliane took hold of one of Melanie's arms. "Come on. I'll introduce you to my aunt Ginny."

Reluctantly, Melanie followed Juliane. Even though Melanie told herself that there was no reason to be nervous, she couldn't help thinking that Nathan's parents came with credentials similar to Tim's parents. But that didn't mean they were like Tim's parents. Prejudging John and Ginny Keller would make her the same as Tim's parents—critical.

As Juliane introduce Melanie to Ginny Keller, the older woman grasped one of Melanie's hands. "I'm so glad to finally meet you. I remember when you started the grief recovery group at church. What a wonderful ministry."

"Thanks." Melanie read the warmth in Ginny's eyes, which were the same color as Nathan's. But Melanie couldn't help wondering whether that warmth would disappear if she found out about Melanie's past. Giving herself a mental shake, she knew she had to quit the negative thinking. But she'd lived with it for years and found it hard to overcome.

"Mom, Mom, the boat's so cool." Andrew ran up to Melanie and pulled on her arm.

Ryan sprinted up next to Andrew. "Nathan said we could go in the boat first."

"That's nice." Melanie looked up to see Nathan, his dad, Seth and Olivia coming their way. Tension tightened her shoulders as she forced herself to put on a calm facade, even though her heart was racing.

"Dad, I want you to meet Ryan and Andrew's mom, Melanie Drake." Nathan smiled at her. "Melanie, this is my dad, John."

"Hello, Mr. Keller." Melanie extended her hand.

"Well, well, well, so this is the little lady who makes the great spaghetti?" John gave her a firm handshake. "And please, call me John."

Tongue-tied, Melanie nodded, then glanced at Nathan as questions bombarded her mind. Had he told his parents about having dinner at her house, or had her boys told Nathan's dad while they were working with the boat? What was she to make of the comment? Was she supposed to brag on her own spaghetti?

Nodding, Nathan grinned. "Her spaghetti is fantastic."

"Yeah, it's the best." Ryan puffed out his chest as if he were the one who made the spaghetti.

Nathan ruffled Ryan's hair. "You got that right."

Laughter rippled through the group, and her tension eased. Taking a deep breath, she followed as everyone trouped back up to the picnic area. Soon the place was teeming with Kellers of every age, and Juliane introduced Melanie to the aunts, uncles and cousin that she hadn't met before.

The men started the charcoal in the built-in barbeque pit, and before long, the scent of burning charcoal mingled with the smell of grilling hamburgers and hot dogs. The women arranged the side dishes on a portable table, while large coolers of iced tea and lemonade sat on the tailgate of a pickup that had been backed up near the tables.

Melanie drank in the conversation and laughter. Everything about this gathering spelled happiness and caring just as Addie

Keller's birthday party had. Closing her eyes, Melanie let the sounds sink into her brain. She shouldn't let the longing start, but the need to belong soaked into her heart and left her wanting what this family had. Lots of love.

Melanie wanted a part of this. Was that possible, or was she setting herself up for more heartache?

Sharing in this family meant welcoming a relationship with Nathan, and dating again meant taking risks. Her boys might have expectations where Nathan was concerned and wind up being disappointed if things didn't work out. She could get hurt herself. Then there was the biggest risk of all—alienating the Drakes and facing the uncertainty involved in any of these scenarios, but as in the financial plans she had talked over with Nathan, rewards didn't come without some risk.

Chapter Seven

In the distance, the buzz of a speedboat made background noise for the birds calling to each other from the treetops. A couple of sailboats glided across the lake, and several wind-surfers guided their boards and colorful sails around the cove near the picnic area.

Melanie took in the picturesque scene as she finished her hot dog. "That was good. Hot dogs cooked on the grill are one of my favorite foods."

"Mine, too." Juliane wiped her hands on her napkin, then glanced at the clearing where Lukas, Seth and Nathan were playing baseball with the kids. "Looks like Ryan and Andrew are having a good time. Nathan has really taken an interest in your boys."

"I know, and I appreciate it." Melanie hoped Juliane wouldn't start hounding her again about Nathan. Even though Melanie was tempted to abandon her reticence concerning him, it was a moot point unless he indicated an interest in her. And that hadn't happened.

Juliane stood. "I'm going to check out the desserts. How about you?"

"I'll pass."

"Okay." As Juliane left, Melanie heard someone approach

from behind her. She turned to look. "Ms. Addie, it's nice to see you again."

"I see my grandson invited you to the family picnic. Good for him."

Smiling at the older woman, Melanie wondered whether it would be worth the bother to set the record straight, but she couldn't let a wrong impression live. "Not your grandson, but your granddaughter Juliane."

Sitting beside Melanie, Addie clasped her hands. "And here I thought he'd wised up. I'll have to talk to him."

Melanie wondered how she could discourage Addie's idea without appearing to dislike Nathan. "Nathan's been very kind to my boys. That's enough."

Leaning forward, Addie gave Melanie a penetrating look. "After the heartbreak of his last relationship, I keep wanting to see him find someone nice to love. I was hoping for more to develop between you two."

Me, too. The thought flitted through Melanie's mind. Whether from the power of suggestion or the magnetic pull of the Keller family's love and devotion to each other, Melanie knew the thought was true. Nathan appealed to her on so many levels—his willingness to help her and the boys, his intelligence and thoughtfulness and his disarming good looks. Despite what she'd said to Juliane, Melanie wanted more than friendship from Nathan. The realization scared her—that risk thing she'd been thinking about. She pushed the thought away, while Addie's comment about Nathan's prior relationship only added to Melanie's questions about Nathan.

"Mom, Mom." Ryan stumbled to a breathless halt. "Nathan says it's time to take out the boat."

"Are they going right this minute?" Melanie surveyed the area. "Are you sure?"

Nodding, he tugged on one of Melanie's arms. "You've gotta come now."

"Is Andrew still with Nathan?"

"Yes. Come on. You've gotta hurry."

Melanie looked over at Addie. "I'm going to have to talk with Nathan about this boat ride. Will you tell Juliane where I've gone?"

Grinning, Addie gave Melanie a knowing look. "Certainly, dear."

Following Ryan, Melanie headed toward the dock, the image of a pleased Addie etched on her brain. Melanie was certain that the older woman's expression meant that she was still hoping for romance to blossom between her grandson and Melanie.

Ryan raced down the dock and stopped at the boat where Melanie could see Nathan and Andrew standing at the stern. Dressed in a pair of red swim trunks and one of those special shirts made for water and sun, Nathan was busy helping his dad and Lukas get life jackets and skis out of a compartment in the bottom of the boat.

"Coach Nathan, here's my mom," Ryan yelled.

Looking up, Nathan grinned. "Hi, Mom. Are you ready to ski?"

"I don't know that I'll be skiing. I just wanted to know what's happening. Ryan seems to think you're leaving this minute." Melanie's pulse raced like the speedboats on the lake.

"No, we're not leaving, yet." Still grinning, Nathan lifted Andrew over the side of the boat and deposited him on the dock. "But it's time to change into your swimsuits."

Melanie tried not to contemplate Nathan's attention to her son. Seeing them together made her think of the two in terms of father and son. She wasn't ready to go there yet. But if someone asked her if she liked Nathan and thought he was handsome, the way her boys had asked Nathan about her, she'd have to say yes, especially when he gave her that lopsided grin and called her Mom. If she were honest with herself, she'd have to admit that he'd had a similar effect on her that day in the bank. "Where do we do that?"

"Up at the bathhouse." Nathan pointed toward the parking lot. "Juliane can show you where it is."

"Thanks." Melanie headed Ryan and Andrew in that direction. "Let's change."

They met Juliane on the way. "Where you guys going?"

"To change." Melanie glanced back at the boat. "Nathan said he's leaving in a few minutes and told me you could tell us where the bathhouse is."

"Sure. Come with me."

Minutes later, Melanie sat in the boat in the seat right behind Nathan, who occupied the co-captain's chair. Juliane sat next to her, while her boys joined the teenagers in the seats at the back of the boat. Melanie was beginning to wonder why Andrew had insisted that she sit near Nathan. Had her little boy turned into a matchmaker, too?

As John Keller maneuvered the boat out into the lake, Melanie, despite her sunglasses, squinted against the brightness of the sun reflecting off the calm water. The air smelled of water, fish and pine forest. She glanced at Andrew and Ryan. They wore their life jackets like badges of honor as they practically bounced in their seats with excitement. No doubt, her boys were basking in the attention of the older kids. She tried to tell herself that this experience was good for them, but she couldn't help worrying about this adventure.

After they reached an open area of the lake, Nathan's dad slowed the boat and shouted over the drone of the motor. "Who wants to ski first?"

A noisy chorus of "me, me" rose from the kids of various ages.

Melanie leaned closer to Juliane. "Do all of these kids ski?"

Juliane nodded. "I told you they've been skiing since they learned to swim."

"If I try to ski, it could be embarrassing." Melanie winced. "I'm pretty sure I'll sit this one out."

"I don't think you have to worry about it for a while. The kids will ski first anyway."

The older kids took turns skiing in the beginning. When they'd each had a turn, Nathan looked at Ryan and Andrew. "Do you boys want to give it try?"

Waving a hand above his head, Andrew jumped up from his seat. "I do."

"Okay. Let's get the trainer skis out." After rummaging around in a compartment in the deck of the boat, Nathan pulled out a pair of skis. Holding them up, Nathan turned to Melanie. "These are especially made for beginners."

"Good." Melanie wanted to be relieved, but even the assurance that others had been successful with the skis didn't calm her nerves.

Nathan slipped the smaller skis off the back of the boat and into the water. He jumped into the water after them and disappeared beneath the surface. Coming up, he wiped the water from his face with one hand. He looked back at Andrew. "Are you ready?"

Andrew nodded. Melanie could almost see his skinny little legs shaking. If she could say no for him, would he be relieved or angry? But she knew there was no way he was going to change his mind. Trying to shake away her fears, she knew she couldn't deny him this opportunity. She had to let her kids experience this new adventure. Nathan wouldn't let Andrew try if he thought it was too dangerous. She had to believe that.

Nathan motioned for Andrew to join him. "Okay, climb down the ladder and swim out to me."

After Andrew joined Nathan in the water, he pushed the

skis ahead of them as they paddled to the end of the ski rope. Nathan helped Andrew put the skis on and put the towrope in his hand. Nathan bobbed in the water behind Andrew and continued to give him instructions, showing him how to hold the rope and keep the skis in place.

"Let us know when you're ready," Juliane called out to them.

After talking with Andrew a minute more, Nathan waved his hand in the air. "Okay."

The boat crept ahead, and the towrope grew taut. Melanie held her breath, her stomach in a knot. Gripping the seat cushion, she closed her eyes for a second. *Lord, please keep my baby safe.*

John opened the throttle, and the boat picked up speed. Melanie opened her eyes just as Andrew popped up out of the water like a jack-in-a-box. Skimming over the glassy surface, he looked so small, but he was skiing. Melanie waved wildly at him like an excited child. Then he listed to one side and fell. The empty towrope trailed behind the boat while Andrew sank into the water.

Melanie covered her mouth with one hand. Was he all right? Then she saw him waving his hand as he bobbed in the water. Taking a deep breath, she put a hand over her heart. He was okay, but was she? Would she survive this?

Juliane patted her shoulder. "Andrew did good for his first time. I think he might be a natural at this."

Melanie took another deep breath. "This is nerve-racking."

"Yeah, I could tell by your white knuckles."

"I was praying the whole time." Melanie stared at Juliane. "And I realized that this is only the beginning of all the things I'm going to have to live through while raising two boys."

Juliane put an arm around Melanie's shoulders. "You'll survive, and prayer is always a good thing."

"Thanks." Melanie managed a smile. As John turned the boat around, Nathan swam to meet Andrew. Although she couldn't tell what Nathan was saying, Andrew nodded. Melanie couldn't put aside her anxiety. "Looks like he wants to make another attempt."

Juliane smiled. "He's a brave little man."

Melanie wished she were a braver mother. During Andrew's next try, he stayed up for several more seconds than the first time, and Melanie's fears eased a little. But her prayers continued. When Andrew climbed the ladder and stepped into the boat, he was all smiles. Melanie gave him a big hug as the older kids cheered.

"Mom, that was so fun. Did you see me?"

"Of course I saw you. You did really well."

Still in the water, Nathan grinned and gave her the thumbs-up sign. "Andrew did super! Is Ryan ready to go?"

Melanie turned to look at Ryan. She saw the worry in his eyes, and she was concerned that he really didn't want to attempt this. But she could also tell that he wasn't going to let his little brother show him up. More anxiety knotted her stomach as she watched Ryan climb down the ladder into the water.

"Okay. We're off." Nathan smiled and waved as he swam off with Ryan.

Melanie smiled in return. Nathan was so good to her boys, and she feared that she was beginning to like him too much. Although she was still nervous as Ryan took his turn, she had confidence that Nathan would guide Ryan in a successful attempt at skiing. A little bigger and a little stronger, Ryan was able to stay up on the skis a minute or so longer than Andrew. Although she was happy for Ryan, she hoped he wouldn't brag about his lengthier ride and make Andrew feel inferior.

When Ryan returned to the boat, a grin split his face as Andrew greeted him with a high five and the older kids cheered again. Melanie was glad to see the brothers sharing their success rather than trying to outdo each other.

"That was fun." Ryan looked at her. "Mom, it's your turn now."

Melanie shook her head. "I think someone else should go. Juliane? Lukas? Nathan?"

"I'll go since I'm already in the water." Nathan motioned for someone to give him the other set of skis.

In minutes, Nathan was skiing with ease as his dad pulled him around the lake. Melanie couldn't take her eyes off him. The ski belt hugged his trim waist, and his broad shoulders were accentuated as he held on to the towrope. He was definitely a handsome man, but more important, he was kind and thoughtful. Melanie remembered what his grandmother had said about the end of a previous relationship. What had caused a woman to break up with a wonderful man like Nathan?

Trying to figure out the answer to that question was only going to get her into deeper trouble. She had to put her thoughts elsewhere. She turned to Juliane. "Are you going to ski next?"

Juliane shook her head. "Oh, no. It's your turn, and I'm not going to let you get out of it like Nathan. So prepare yourself."

Melanie stewed while Nathan continued to ski. Her only hope was that he would never stop. *Wishful thinking.*

After Nathan finished skiing without the slightest hint that he would fall, he climbed back into the boat. Grabbing a beach towel, he looked right at her as he dried off. "I've been told you're going to go next."

Melanie figured she might as well not fight the general consensus that it was her turn. She took a deep breath. "I guess, but remember I haven't been water-skiing in a long time. So go easy, okay?"

Nathan gave her a salute. "Will do."

Cinching her life vest tighter, she hoped this wouldn't be a disaster. She climbed down the ladder and eased herself into the water. Winking, Nathan slid her the skis. "You'll do fine."

Her heart fluttered. "I hope so."

"Ryan and Andrew are cheering you on."

As she put on the skis, her boys peered at her over the side of the boat. Taking a deep breath, she took the towrope and squared herself in the water. The rope tightened as John slowly drove the boat forward.

Nathan waved. "Let us know when you're ready."

Melanie waved her hand. She squeezed the towrope and said a little prayer. She felt the pull of the rope on her arms as she rose out of the water. A sense of euphoria gripped her as she skimmed along the calm surface without difficulty. She was actually skiing. She hadn't forgotten how to do it.

She could see Ryan, Andrew and Nathan watching her. Her boys were clapping. She forgot to be nervous until she crossed the wake of the boat. She looked down and her legs flew out from under her as she fell unceremoniously into the water. Sputtering to the surface, she waved to let them know she was all right while the boat circled back to her.

"You have to go again," Nathan called as the boat stopped beside her. "This time relax and bend your knees when you go over the wake."

Melanie slowly shook her head. "I'm not going again."

"Once more. You don't want to give up now." His voice held a challenge. "The kids say you have to try again."

Ryan and Andrew started yelling, and soon everyone in the boat was chanting, "Go, Mom. Go, Mom. Go, Mom."

Smiling with resignation, Melanie grabbed the rope and maneuvered into position. "Okay. One more time, and that's all."

In seconds, she was out of the water again. Breezing along

behind the boat, she was content not to cross the wake. Nathan motioned with his hand for her to cut over, but she ignored him. She stared down at the foaming water and the ridge that separated her from the smooth water outside the wake. Maybe considering a relationship with Nathan was like crossing the wake. Maybe both were challenges worth taking.

With a deep breath and knees relaxed, she slowly eased her skis toward the edge of the foaming water. Determined to make it, she let the skis glide over the ridge, and when she was still upright, she grinned and waved at the cheering group at the back of the boat. Would getting over the humps in her relationship with Nathan be this easy?

At everyone's urging, she crossed to the other side of the wake, then back again. Gaining confidence, she went back and forth several times, finding the experience exhilarating. Without warning, they crossed the wake of another boat, and she lost her balance. Leaning forward, she tried to regain her equilibrium. Finally, realizing she wasn't going to make it, she dropped the rope and immediately plunged into the lake again.

When the boat pulled up beside her, Nathan leaning over the side with a concerned expression. "You okay?"

Melanie nodded and paddled to the ladder. "That's it for me."

Nathan held out his hand. "You did fine, despite that last spill."

"I suspect I'll have some sore muscles in the morning." Melanie tried not to think about Nathan's warm, strong hand gripping hers as he helped her aboard.

Before she could sit down, Nathan was beside her as he held out a towel. "Here. Put this around you."

His attention made her pulse race. She hoped he couldn't hear her heart that seemed to thunder over the drone of the boat's motor. Quickly returning to her seat, she averted her gaze fearing that Nathan might read her reaction to him in her eyes. She feared that Juliane was taking in the whole episode with more matchmaking on her mind.

As she snuggled into the towel, Ryan and Andrew swarmed all over her. She gave them each a hug. "I'm glad that's over."

Eying her, Ryan stood up tall. "But, Mom, you were good—almost as good as Nathan."

"I hardly think so. And Nathan probably doesn't agree with that, either." Shaking her head, Melanie chuckled.

Nathan turned to face Melanie and winked. "Of course, you're almost as good as I am, and with a little practice, you could be a great skier."

"Well, there are a few problems. I don't have a boat or skis or time to practice." Melanie laughed.

Juliane leaned toward Melanie. "Nathan could take you out every weekend for some practice."

Nathan shook his head. "Not any time soon. We're in the middle of a bank audit. The examiners are there every day, and I'm trying to gauge what's going on with them. The bank is about all I'm thinking about these days."

Melanie wondered if Nathan's excuse not to help her meant that he didn't want to be with her. Chiding herself mentally, she dismissed the thought. She didn't know why she was thinking in those terms anyway. He'd never indicated a romantic interest in her. When was she going to quit letting other people like Juliane and Addie put crazy ideas in her head?

While Melanie worked to get her thoughts on a sensible track, Lukas and Juliane each took a turn skiing. Even John made one run while Nathan drove the boat. Then the teens skied again. Ryan and Andrew also skied another time, each doing a little better than their first outing. As the sun sank lower in the sky, John turned the boat back toward the dock.

After the boat arrived at the dock, everyone disembarked.

Nathan, Lukas, John and a couple of the teenage boys stayed behind to get the boat back on the trailer. Melanie and the others made their way back to the picnic area where they changed clothes in the bathhouse.

While the sun sank slowly behind the trees surrounding the lake, several men played horseshoes, and others played checkers or chess. Addie and a group of ladies sat at a table where they were involved in an intense game of dominoes. Watching the laughter and camaraderie, Melanie couldn't help wanting to be a permanent part of this picture, not just a guest. Besides all the wonderful qualities she saw in Nathan, her thoughts about Nathan were all wrapped up in her longing for family. But wishing and reality were two different things.

Ryan and Andrew joined in one of the board games, while Melanie took in the beauty of her surroundings. The water reflected the fiery orange glow in the sky. Quiet conversation mingled with the chirp of crickets in the early evening air. A distant motorboat buzzed, accompanying the sound of water lapping at the rocky shoreline. The smell of burning charcoal once again filled the air as several men began preparing the barbeque pit to cook the evening meal. Soon the area was abuzz with food preparation.

While Melanie drank in the peaceful surroundings, Barbara and Ginny joined her. Melanie turned to greet them. "Hi. This is quite an occasion. I had no idea you made such a huge production out of a picnic."

Barbara smiled. "We Kellers like to have a good time, so we always make a day of it when we get together."

"Did Nathan teach your boys to water-ski?" Ginny asked.

"He did, and they loved it." Melanie chuckled. "He's a very good teacher."

Ginny nodded. "He's always been good with kids. I wish

he'd spend more weekends like this—just enjoying life. He works too hard, and I worry about his health."

Melanie wondered what Ginny meant by the statement about Nathan's health but didn't want to ask for fear that she would appear to be nosy. "Is there anything you'd like me to do to help get ready for supper?"

Barbara shook her head. "The guys are taking care of it. They're grilling the steaks, and we have potato salad and coleslaw to go with them. And watermelon for dessert."

"Sounds good." Melanie looked up just in time to see Nathan approaching. Little sparks seemed to jump in her chest.

"Hey." He put an arm around his mom's shoulders. "We got the boat back on the trailer. What did you and Aunt Barbara do this afternoon?"

"A bunch of us spent our time working on the quilts for the nursing home."

Nathan grimaced. "That makes the rest of us sound like slackers."

Ginny shook her head. "Hardly. You love to ski, and we love to quilt. We were both doing things we love."

"Okay. You're making me feel not so guilty. I'd better go help with the food preparation." Nathan looked at Melanie. "I told the boys I'd save space for the three of you at my table. See you there."

"Okay." Melanie relished the invitation even though it was meant more for her boys than it was for her.

"I can't believe I made him feel guilty for having fun. He needs to do more of that." Sighing, Ginny glanced at Melanie. "I hope your boys will help him do that."

"I'm sure Ryan and Andrew will be more than eager to help him. They think he's the greatest. Around our house these days, it's Coach Nathan said this, and Coach Nathan said that."

"Well, baseball is the one thing that gets him away from work, and sometimes even that doesn't." Ginny took a deep breath. "I smell those steaks. We'd better get ready to eat."

"Okay. I'm going to round up my kids." Melanie spied Ryan and Andrew still playing a game with some of the older boys. As she wandered over to where they sat, she couldn't get the conversation with Nathan's mother out of her mind. What drove Nathan to work all the time, and why was his mother worried about his health? These were two more questions to add to the one her talk with Nathan's grandmother had prompted.

Melanie wondered whether she'd ever find an answer to those questions. Would Nathan allow her to get close enough to learn more about him?

When the steaks were ready, one of Nathan's uncles said a prayer. Afterward, folks lined up to get their food. Melanie went through the serving line with Ryan and Andrew, who were anxious to eat with Nathan. As soon as the boys had their food, they headed straight for the table where Nathan sat with his parents. Melanie hesitated. How was she going to deal with John and Ginny Keller? They'd been very nice to her so far, but her experience with Tim's parents so often colored her dealings with people she considered superior to her.

Melanie stood back for a minute and watched Ryan and Andrew settle in at the table. Thankfully, her boys didn't have her inferior attitudes. She wanted to make sure they never felt that way. Nathan greeted them with a smile. His dad said something to Ryan, then gave him a high five. Andrew reached up his little hand to receive a high five also. Melanie wondered what that was all about, but she was glad to see that her sons were accepted. She never wanted them to feel abandoned or left out as she had been while growing up.

As she drew closer to the table, Nathan looked up and

smiled at her. Their eyes met. Her insides jumbled with a feeling similar to the one she'd had while skiing just before she realized she was going to fall. Was she falling again? This whole day had been filled with warning signs that she was doing exactly that—falling for Nathan Keller.

Melanie wanted to hold tight to all the reasons for not letting that happen just as she'd gripped the towrope in an effort to keep herself from plunging into the water. But in the end, she'd succumbed to natural forces. Was she fighting a losing battle again? She pushed the question away as she sat beside Ryan.

"Hi, Mom. What took you so long?" Ryan stabbed a piece of steak with his fork.

"I didn't take long. You guys were just too fast for me. Must be that baseball practice."

Andrew nodded. "That's it. We're getting so fast because Coach Nathan makes us run the bases three times at the beginning of every practice."

"That must be it." Melanie chuckled as she glanced at Nathan, who was sitting directly across the table from her.

Nathan grinned. "That's got to be it. You boys are getting too fast."

"Nathan, speaking of baseball. The bank has four tickets for the Reds game on Wednesday, and no one has stepped forward to use them. You should take these two young men." John looked at Ryan and Andrew. "What do you think, boys?"

"Can our mom come, too?" Andrew looked over at Melanie.

Her stomach sinking, Melanie saw the trapped look in Nathan's eyes. Andrew had done it again. Was her son deliberately pushing her and Nathan together, or was it only an innocent suggestion? Either way, she had to let Nathan off the hook. "I'm not sure I'll be done with work in time to go, but you boys can go. That should be lots of fun."

Nathan narrowed his gaze. "I'm not sure I can go, either, Dad. You know the audit's in full swing. I'm in Seth's wedding, and we're already going to a Reds game on Thursday night for his bachelor party. Then there's the rehearsal on Friday and the wedding on Saturday, not to mention that we play our first youth baseball games this week. That doesn't leave me much extra time."

"Son, go have some fun. You've done fine work getting your people in place to deal with the bank examiners. Trust them to do a good job." John glanced at Ginny. "Your mom and I have been off having fun. It's your turn. Take these little guys and their mother to the game. Besides, we don't want those tickets to go to waste."

Melanie could see indecision in Nathan's expression, and hope in her sons' eyes. She didn't care about the baseball game for herself, but she wanted this for Ryan and Andrew. John had raised the boys' expectations about seeing a major league baseball game, and she didn't want them to be disappointed.

Shrugging, Nathan looked at his dad, then at Ryan and Andrew. "I don't know, guys. Let me see how things go at the beginning of the week. If no one has taken the tickets by the time we have our first game on Tuesday night, I'll take you to the game. How about that?"

Andrew nodded. "I'm going to pray that no one else wants the tickets."

Leave it to Andrew to say exactly what was on his mind. There was never any doubt where you stood with that child—good or bad. Melanie couldn't help thinking that this was all part of the inevitability of spending time with Nathan that she'd thought about while skiing.

Chapter Eight

The noise of the crowd filtered around them as Nathan led Melanie and her boys to a field-level section along the first base line in the Great American Ball Park. Gloves in hand, Ryan and Andrew could hardly contain their excitement as they stopped at the top of the steps that led down to their seats. A look of awe crept across their little faces as they surveyed the baseball diamond in the home of the Cincinnati Reds. For the first time since they'd left home tonight, they were speechless.

Nathan tried to remember his own excitement and sense of awe during his first Reds game more than twenty-five years ago. Of course, back then, the games were played in the old Riverfront Stadium, which had been demolished and replaced several years ago with this new ballpark. He'd been about Andrew's age when his dad and Grandpa Watkins had taken him and his brother to see the Reds play the Chicago Cubs. He could still remember the score. The Reds had won seven to three. That experience served to cement his love for baseball.

Nathan glanced over at Melanie, who had been unusually quiet during the ride to Cincinnati while she'd occupied the front passenger seat. Or maybe she'd never had a chance to say anything because Ryan and Andrew talked nearly nonstop, as their exuberant chatter filled the backseat. Either way, he worried that she'd only come because her sons had made the invitation. Nathan feared that she wasn't nearly as excited to be here.

"Let's find our seats." Nathan studied the tickets. "Looks like we're in row L down this aisle."

As they descended the steps, Nathan realized that he used to know right where the bank seats were located, but not anymore. The bank had purchased season tickets since before he was born, and Nathan had used his share to entertain clients or attend a game just because no one else had claimed the tickets that were shared by the bank employees. Sadly, he began to see how he'd buried himself in his work at the bank, so much so, that he'd given up one of his favorite pastimes—watching baseball.

"Here's our row. Row L." Ryan skipped into the row and claimed his seat.

Andrew raced in behind Ryan, then looked back at Melanie. "Mom, you can sit next to me."

"You mean you don't want to sit next to Coach Nathan?"

Andrew shook his head. "I want to sit next to you, and you can sit next to Coach. That way you can learn about baseball from both of us."

"Okay." Melanie sat next to Andrew, then looked up at Nathan as she appeared to be holding back a smile. "Is that okay with you?"

"That works for me." Nathan's gaze fell on the hint of a smile curving Melanie's mouth, the first one he'd seen all evening. He quickly turned away because looking at her lips made him think about kissing her. He'd had that same thought when he'd been at the club helping her with her financial portfolio. Since then, he managed to keep thoughts like those at bay, but tonight they'd slipped unguarded into his mind, like a runner stealing a base. He had to think of something else. "Anyone want something to eat besides me?"

"Me, me." Both boys jumped up.

"Okay. I'll take orders and go get some food."

Melanie gazed up at Nathan. "Are you going to be able to bring it back by yourself?"

Nathan nodded. "Probably. They'll give me one of those things to carry everything in."

"Okay, but one of the boys can help you if you need it."

"Can we both help?" Ryan asked.

"Sure." Nathan looked at Melanie and realized he'd spoken out of turn. He'd given permission without asking her first. "Um…that's if it's okay with your mom."

"Yeah, it's okay." Melanie took hold of Ryan's arm as he passed in front of her. "You stay right with Coach Nathan, and do whatever he says. Do you understand?"

Both boys nodded. Then Andrew gave her a hug. "Mom, don't be lonely without us."

Melanie ruffled his hair. "Thanks, Andrew. I'll be fine. Bring me back a really good hot dog."

"I will." Andrew joined Ryan and Nathan on the steps, then turned back to Melanie. "Watch our gloves."

"Okay. I'll take good care of them." Melanie waved.

While the boys climbed the steps ahead of Nathan, he couldn't help imagining that this was what it would be like to have a wife and children of his own. Why had he let his mind take him there again? The answer wasn't too hard to figure out. He liked the feeling, but, at the same time, he was running scared from that very emotion—the one he'd first experienced at the Dairy Barn after baseball practice. Could he ever conquer his fear and discover the possibilities with Melanie?

The question plagued Nathan while he placed his order, and it continued to occupy his thoughts as they started back to their seats loaded down with their food. Nathan carried the drinks, and Ryan and Andrew each carried a bag containing the hot dogs, chips and condiments. Would he ever be brave enough to actually ask Melanie for a date, or would he keep using events like this to be with her?

His thoughts about Melanie that night at the Dairy Barn had crystallized his feelings for her, causing him to panic. After practices the following week, he'd refused to go with everyone to the Dairy Barn, making his excuses and going home. But during the days since the family picnic, he'd started to rethink his reaction. Maybe he was being stupid to try to run away from his feelings. Was that admission the first step in figuring out what he wanted?

Carefully balancing the drinks, Nathan watched Ryan and Andrew scamper ahead as he made his way down the aisle steps. "Boys, slow down and hang right here with me. I can't go as fast as you with these drinks."

Slowing down, Andrew turned. "Okay, Coach.

Nathan breathed a sigh of relief when Ryan did the same. The seats were beginning to fill up, as the crowd grew larger. Nathan couldn't imagine the real panic if he lost one of these kids. The realization made him think about the responsibilities of family life—the part that went beyond sharing laughter and having fun. Surprisingly the thought didn't scare him. If he could think in those terms about Ryan and Andrew, why did he hold back when it came to Melanie?

Fear. Could he take a chance on love, when she might reject him because of his health issues?

"We're back." Nathan let the boys into the row, then looked down at Melanie. She smiled. His heart tripped, and he almost dropped the drinks.

"That didn't take too long." She reached up to him. "I'll pass the drinks down to the kids."

"Thanks." Nathan handed her two of the cups, then settled

beside her in his aisle seat. He pushed aside his troubling thoughts and helped pass out the hot dogs and chips. "Good thing we beat the crowd."

"I'm glad I was able to get off work a little early." Melanie pulled on her hot-pink top. "You're probably surprised to see me in something besides scrubs."

"I see you on Sundays, and you're not wearing scrubs."

"That doesn't count."

"It doesn't?" Nathan chuckled. "Actually, I kind of like the ones you wear with the dancing toothbrushes."

"Then I'll have to remember to wear those on game days." She grinned at him.

Did she mean she intended to wear those scrubs because he liked them? Was she flirting with him, or was his imagination working overtime? He wasn't sure he could tell. He hadn't flirted with a woman in years. Trying to think of something else, Nathan looked over at the boys. "How are the hot dogs?"

Nodding, they mumbled their approval while their eyes were trained on the players throwing the ball around the infield.

"Why do hot dogs from a ballpark always taste so good?" Melanie licked a blob of mustard off one finger.

"Maybe it's the atmosphere." Nathan couldn't help thinking that even her actions had a flirtatious element to them. Nathan quickly shook away that thought. Now he knew his imagination was out of control. She was eating a hot dog—not flirting with him in front of her children.

"Maybe I just love hot dogs." Melanie laughed and the sound went straight to Nathan's heart. "They were really good at the picnic last weekend, too."

"I'll go with your spaghetti."

"Since you like my spaghetti so much, I'll have to fix my manicotti for you sometime."

"Is that an invitation for supper?"

"If you'd like one." Taking a sip of her drink, she looked at him over the top of the cup.

"This is one invitation I can't pass up."

"So when aren't you busy?"

Melanie's question said everything about his life. He'd stuffed it full of activities, but he'd taken them for granted by just putting in his time—at church, at family gatherings, even at baseball practice. Never letting any of those occasions bring him the joy he used to feel. He'd been going through the motions—even with the baseball that he loved. Convincing himself that his work at the bank was what he lived for, he'd worked long hours but with little satisfaction. He was determined to make some changes. Setting a date for this dinner without looking at his calendar was going to be a start. "How about a week from Saturday?"

"I'll plan on it." Melanie pulled a little cell phone out of her purse and flipped it open. The phone emitted little beeping sounds as she put his name into the calendar. "What time?"

"You tell me, and I'll be there."

"Six-thirty."

"It's a date."

Was this a date? The question popped into Nathan's mind—a question he couldn't answer. While she finished putting the information into the phone's calendar, Nathan wondered why she'd so readily asked him to dinner. Was this a friendly gesture or something more? He shouldn't read anything into it. She probably considered him only a friend. Or maybe she felt as though she needed to do something to pay him back for bringing them to the game. She'd tried to pay him for the tickets, but he'd refused. He should take the invitation at face value.

Why was he tying himself in knots over a simple request to have some of her great cooking? If he really wanted to know the answer to his question, he would ask her out on a real date—one where just the two of them would have an evening together, instead of using baseball practice, family gatherings or his father's prompting to take her boys to a baseball game. When was he going to do that? He finally realized that he was ready to move on and try to find love again, putting aside his past heartache.

Nathan's vexing thoughts came to an end as an announcement blared over the stadium's sound system, requesting everyone to stand for the "National Anthem."

When the anthem was over cheers filled the stadium and Ryan punched his glove. "I'm ready to catch a foul ball, like I caught that ball in our game the other night."

"Me, too." Andrew imitated his older brother. "Do you think they'll hit one in our direction?"

"There's a good chance." Nathan settled in his seat. "You guys played a really good game on Tuesday. I'm proud of you. Now we have two wins and no losses."

"Thanks, Coach." Andrew punched his glove again. "I'm going to catch a ball just like a big league outfielder."

"I hope you do." Melanie patted him on the head. "Because I'll be ducking if a ball heads my way."

"Mom, you don't have to worry. I'll protect you with my glove." Andrew puffed out his chest.

One of the Reds players smacked a ball into left field for a double, and the crowd roared. Ryan and Andrew jumped up and cheered. Ryan looked over at Melanie and Nathan. "Dad used to hit the ball that far, didn't he, Mom?

Melanie nodded. "He was a very good ball player. He told me that some pro scouts came to look at him while he was playing college baseball."

Nathan couldn't help thinking how Ryan and Andrew remembered all the good things about their dad. He was their hero. That gave Nathan pause. If he developed a relationship with Melanie, would he find himself always compared to Tim Drake? Another question to add to his growing list.

"I'm going to practice hard so I can hit one that far, too." Ryan pretended to swing a bat.

Melanie chuckled. "You have some growing up to do first."

"I'm going to get big and strong like Dad." Ryan clenched his fists and held up his arms like a weight lifter flexing his muscles.

"Me, too." Andrew again imitated Ryan.

"Okay, you two, let's watch—"

"Look out, guys, here comes a foul ball." Nathan pointed toward the sky.

Looking upward, Ryan and Andrew both held up their gloves as the ball descended toward their seats. True to her word, Melanie ducked and covered her head with her arms. The ball hit the hands of a man sitting in front of them, bounced off the man's hands right into Ryan's glove.

Ryan plucked it out of his glove and held it up high as he jumped up and down. He yelled at the top of his lungs. "I caught the foul ball."

Folks seated around them cheered and patted him on the back. He was grinning from ear to ear.

"Can I see it?" Andrew's expression held a hint of awe mingled with some disappointment.

"Don't drop it." Ryan reluctantly handed it to his little brother.

"Cool." After carefully inspecting the ball, Andrew shoved it under Melanie's nose. "Look at this, Mom."

Melanie straightened after her imitation of a duck-and-cover drill. "Yes, that's very nice. What are you going to do with it?"

"Can I put it on the shelf with Dad's trophies?" Ryan held out his hand to retrieve the ball from Andrew.

Melanie reached over and took the ball before he could give it back to Ryan. "Let me put this in my purse for safekeeping. That way you won't lose it, and your hands will be free to catch another one."

Andrew's face brightened. "Do you think another one will come by us?"

Nathan shrugged. "You never know. Sometimes, it happens that way."

The rest of the game proceeded with more hits, strikeouts and loud cheers. Nathan tried to pay attention, but the lovely woman beside him claimed more of his attention than baseball, despite his love for the game. While the teams battled on the field, he battled with himself about the wisdom of asking Melanie for a date. The idea was never far from his thoughts.

When the game finally ended, the Reds had won five to two. As they left the stadium, the boys were loaded down with souvenirs and full of junk food. Again Nathan's thoughts were filled with ideas of family while they walked to his vehicle. Was he setting himself up for more heartache? He wished he knew.

Sighing, Andrew trudged beside Melanie. "Ryan's lucky cuz he caught a foul ball. I wish I woulda caught one. Can we come to another game sometime, so I have a chance to catch a foul ball?"

"Maybe…later in the summer." Melanie patted the top of Andrew's head.

Andrew looked up at Melanie, then over at Nathan. "I want Coach to come, too. Can he?"

"That would be fun." Nathan wondered whether another baseball game with the kids could count as the date he'd been thinking about. But he knew the answer to his own thought. No. But another baseball game was drawing him closer into their circle—a circle that was beginning to feel more and more comfortable.

When they arrived back at Melanie's house, she glanced in the backseat as Nathan pulled his SUV into the driveway. "Looks like Ryan and Andrew are sound asleep."

"Do you want to wake them?"

Melanie shrugged. "Probably. I don't know how else to get them into the house."

"We could try to carry them." Nathan peered at her in the dim glow coming from the porch light and the nearby streetlamp. "Do you think you can carry Andrew, since he's smaller?"

"I suppose we can give that a try, but first let me unlock the front door."

"Sure." Nathan unbuckled the seat belt that held Ryan in his booster seat. Things were certainly different now. When he was a kid, there were no laws about having booster seats for kids this age.

"Okay, the front door is open. You can go ahead and take Ryan in." Melanie opened the back door of Nathan's SUV. "I'll wait for you, so I know where to take him."

She unbuckled the seat belt and lifted Andrew out. He didn't awaken as she held him against her shoulder.

Doing the same with Ryan, Nathan joined her on the front walk. Ryan's dead weight was heavy as Nathan climbed the steps, and he wondered how Melanie was managing even though Andrew was much slighter. Once inside, Nathan followed her to the left past a bathroom.

Melanie stopped in the hallway and nodded her head toward the second doorway on her left. She mouthed the words. "Lay him on the bed in there."

Nathan nodded, and Melanie continued toward the next doorway. He entered the room lit only by the light coming from the hallway. He smiled when he saw the baseball-themed bedding. He wondered whether he should pull back the covers before placing Ryan on the bed. The boy still hadn't stirred, his weight getting heavier in Nathan's arms.

While Nathan stood there contemplating his next move, Melanie came into the room. She looked up at him and whispered, "I'll pull back the covers."

Nathan nodded. After Melanie had the bed ready, Nathan lowered Ryan onto it.

Again, Melanie kept her voice barely above a whisper. "I'm going to take off his shoes and let him sleep in his clothes tonight. Better than waking him up. I did the same with Andrew."

Nathan slipped into the hallway where he watched her taking care of her son. The domestic scene touched his heart, and a lump rose in his throat. He didn't know why. Maybe because she was a single mom with all the responsibilities for these little guys, or maybe because his feelings for her—and for the boys—were growing minute by minute.

When she was done, she smiled up at him as she joined him in the hallway. "Thanks. You were a big help."

"I was glad to do it."

"Even though you have to go to a baseball game again tomorrow night?" Melanie asked as she headed back toward the entry hall.

"I don't think going to another game will be a hardship." Chuckling, Nathan followed. "But I doubt that I'll have as much fun. There's nothing like being with little boys while they experience their first pro baseball game."

"Oh, they did have a fabulous time. Can we ever top Ryan catching that foul ball?"

"I hope Andrew isn't too disappointed if he doesn't get one. It's not an everyday occurrence to catch a foul ball."

Melanie sighed. "I know. Do you suppose he might forget over time?"

"No. Never."

"That's what I was afraid of." Melanie made a move toward the front door. "We'd better take those booster seats out of your car before we forget."

"Good thinking." Nathan followed Melanie to his SUV.

While they worked to take out the booster seats, Nathan looked at Melanie from the other side of his SUV. Watching her stirred something deep inside of him. He tried to ignore it. "Where do you want this?"

"You can set it in the front hall. I'll put them in my car tomorrow morning."

"Why leave it till tomorrow? I'll help tonight."

"Are you sure? It's already late, and the next couple of days are going to be really busy for you, aren't they?"

"Yeah. Bachelor party, rehearsal, rehearsal dinner and wedding, but I'm used to that. Someone in our family is always getting married. I've about worn out my tux." Nathan laughed, but the talk of weddings set his mind abuzz.

Even though it was short notice, he thought about asking Melanie if he could escort her to Seth and Elise's wedding. The question sat on the tip of his tongue, but he chickened out. She was going to be there whether he asked to escort her or not. Carrying the booster seat, he shoved the idea away and followed her back into the house.

Melanie flipped on the light as she entered the garage. The two cars occupying the space reminded Nathan that one of them had belonged to Tim—the restored Ford Mustang that Ryan had talked about. If Nathan decided to pursue a relationship with Melanie, would he always see constant reminders of her late husband?

While he helped her put the booster seats back into her car, his thoughts swirled with a dozen ways he could ask her out. Little speeches ran through his head, but he dismissed every one of them as inadequate. Why was he letting his experience with Andrea intimidate him? He reminded himself that Melanie wasn't anything like Andrea, but even that didn't help. The fear was winning.

After they finished putting the boosters back into Melanie's car, he accompanied her back into the house. "I'd better be heading home."

"You were so nice to take us to the ball game, especially since you have such a busy weekend ahead of you. I know the boys will never forget it." She walked toward the front hall.

Opening the door, Nathan wanted to ask Melanie whether *she* would ever forget it, but he tamped down the thought. "Guess I'll see you at the wedding."

"I'll be there. Thanks again."

The battle between his fear and his longings escalated in his mind. He looked into her dark-brown eyes, then took in the curve of her mouth. Every nerve hummed. He had to get out of there before he did something stupid like pull her into his arms and kiss her. He wasn't ready for anything like that, and she certainly wouldn't be expecting it. Turning, he opened the door. "Good night."

As he jogged to his SUV, her sweet good-night echoed in his brain. What was he going to do with his ever-growing feelings for Melanie Drake? He should ask her for a real date. He just had to find the right time.

Chapter Nine

Joy swirled through the room as Nathan stood off to one side and watched Seth and Elise cut their cake. Their wedding had gone off without a hitch—one of the few problem-free ceremonies he'd seen in a lifetime of Kellerville weddings. Even though Seth's little girl Olivia had been trouble at the rehearsal, she'd performed her duties as flower girl without a misstep.

But seeing Seth and Elise's happiness heightened the longing Nathan had been feeling ever since the night he'd taken Melanie and her boys to the ball game—maybe ever since the night she'd fed him her great spaghetti. And the spaghetti had nothing to do with the particular emotion that confused him.

The whole atmosphere of a wedding, more than any other family event, served to remind him that he was single. Like being stuck at the kids' table as a teenager during Thanksgiving dinner, weddings made him feel out of place. Nathan remembered how he'd had to sit at the table with the old folks at Lukas and Juliane's wedding reception because he hadn't bothered to bring a date. At least tonight, he was part of the wedding party and seated at a table with people near his own age.

As Nathan watched Elise getting ready to throw the bouquet, Lukas walked his way. "I thought I'd join you while Juliane's busy rounding up the single women for this little exercise."

"Your wife can be a little coercive."

"Hey, that's the love of my life you're talking about there. Be nice. Besides, she's the matron of honor. That's her job."

"And she's doing it very well."

Nodding, Lukas chuckled. "I'm still not believing that Elise decided to have this great big wedding. The whole time Juliane and I were planning our wedding, Elise vowed that she would elope when she decided to get married and avoid all the trouble."

"But in the end, she couldn't deny her family and friends the opportunity to share this day and her happiness."

Lukas slowly nodded, giving Nathan a serious look. "Yeah, that's one thing I've learned living here in Kellerville. Family is important."

"You know I love Juliane and Elise as if they were my kid sisters. They've always been more like sisters than cousins to me."

"That's why they're always looking out for your interests."

Nathan wasn't quite sure what Lukas was getting at with that statement, so he wasn't going to ask. His stomach somersaulted when he noticed Juliane escorting Melanie to the group of women standing in the center of the dance floor. "Some of those ladies don't appear to be very interested in catching the bouquet. Looks to me as though they're out there just putting in an appearance to please Juliane and Elise."

"That's probably true," Lukas said as Elise flung the bouquet over her head toward the crowd of women behind her. One of the younger ones from Seth's family snagged the bouquet and joyously held it high. "I guess that young lady foiled Juliane's plot to get the bouquet to Melanie Drake."

"Is that so?" Nathan tried to feign indifference to the mention of Melanie's name. He hadn't forgotten that this was the anniversary of the day she'd met Tim. During the ceremony she'd been sitting where he couldn't see her. Other than the brief encounter during the reception line, he hadn't had a chance to talk to her. He'd barely seen her during most of the reception up until now. Wondering how she was coping, he wished he'd gone with his heart instead of his brain and asked to escort her, but he couldn't go back and do it over. He'd let the opportunity pass him by.

Lukas clapped Nathan on the back, startling him from his thoughts. "So are you ready to take your shot at catching the garter? After all, I think Seth will be aiming your way."

"No. I've caught more than my share of garters over the years, and so far, I haven't come close to the altar."

"Well, it's time to put in your appearance like those women we were just watching." Lukas gave Nathan a friendly nudge toward the center of the room.

Hoots and hollers filled the room as Seth removed the garter. As he got ready to throw it, he looked in Nathan's direction. Nathan grinned but made no attempt to catch it as it flew through the air. A distant cousin from out of town that Nathan barely knew came away with the garter.

Lukas joined Nathan as he walked back to the table. "Garter or no garter, I'm thinking your marriage prospects are looking up."

"Not you, too." Nathan narrowed his gaze as the disc jockey announced a line dance, and a gaggle of women and a couple of brave men crowded the floor. "Has Juliane been talking to you?"

"About what?"

Nathan didn't know whether Lukas was being intentionally

obtuse or whether he didn't know about Juliane's matchmaking. If Lukas didn't have a clue about Melanie, then Nathan didn't want to bring it up. "I guess she hasn't."

"I could make a good guess." Lukas grinned as he raised his voice over the music. "I'm thinking this has something to do with Melanie Drake."

"And you're basing this on what?" Nathan hoped Lukas's raised voice didn't carry over the music.

Shaking his head, Lukas gave Nathan a knowing look. "I'd have to be blind not to see your interest in Melanie."

Had his interest been that obvious? "Why do you say that?"

"Should I make a list? Spaghetti dinner at her house. Helping her boys with baseball. Having her boys on the bank's team. Coming to the Dairy Barn after practice. Teaching her boys to water-ski. Taking them to the baseball game." Lukas ticked off the things on his fingers. "Since I moved here two and a half years ago, I've never seen you spend so much time on something other than bank business and a family gathering here and there."

Nathan knew there was no sense in denying everything Lukas had pointed out. "Okay, you got me, but let me do this in my own time. Don't push like Juliane."

"I know what you're going through. I was afraid to ask Juliane out at first." Lukas clapped Nathan on the back again. "At least ask Melanie to dance."

"I've got two left feet. I'd be stepping on her toes." Shaking his head, Nathan glanced toward the dance floor. Melanie was out there, moving up and back, turning around and clapping her hands with the other line dancers. He was glad she was having a good time. "There's no way I could begin to follow all those steps."

"Try a slow dance."

"I don't see you dancing."

Lukas eyed Nathan. "Okay. Let's make a deal. During the next slow dance, I'll have Juliane out there, and I'll expect to see you with Melanie."

Nathan decided his time to be brave had come. "Okay. Deal."

Nathan sat at the table with Lukas and watched the same group of women dance to a variety of new and old fast songs. "Do you suppose the disc jockey has no slow songs on his play list?"

"Eager to get out there?" Lukas grinned. "I could make a request."

"No. The deal was the next slow dance. No pushing the agenda."

Lukas laughed halfheartedly. "Okay, but I'd like to dance with my wife instead of watching her dance with a bunch of women."

"But they're having so much fun."

When the rock-and-roll song ended, the disc jockey announced the song "All My Life," a duet sung by Linda Ronstadt and Aaron Neville. Standing, Lukas gave Nathan a nod as he headed to the dance floor to claim Juliane. Taking a deep breath, Nathan followed. As the husbands partnered with their wives and several young men asked their girlfriends to dance, Melanie headed off the dance floor.

His heart pounding, Nathan approached her. "Hey, Melanie."

Stopping, she turned. A smile lit her face when she saw him. "Hi, Nathan. I haven't seen much of you this evening."

Her smile seemed to turn him inside out. He knew he'd better ask her to dance now before he lost his nerve. "I know, and I want to change that. Would you like to dance?"

Her smile broadened. "Yes, I'd like that."

"Let's go." Nathan held out his hand, and she placed her hand in his. As he led her to the dance floor, he hoped he could remember those dance lessons he'd taken in middle school. He'd danced very little in his thirty-four years, and at least half of those times were in dance class—the other half when he'd been unable to avoid dancing at family weddings. Or maybe he should apologize ahead of time for stepping on her toes.

When they reached the dance floor, he put an arm around her waist and pulled her closer. She smiled up at him as she placed a hand on his shoulder. Everything appeared brighter, the music sweeter and the dance floor made just for them. They started moving to the music.

Swallowing a lump in his throat, he tried to relax. He was supposed to be enjoying this experience, but the tension in his body was making it nearly impossible. Should he talk or remain silent? Maybe talking would take his mind off the dancing, but if he didn't concentrate, he'd be sure to step on her toes.

Finally, the words of the song penetrated the fog of his anxiety. Was he wearing his heart on his sleeve as the song said? Had he been looking for Melanie all of his life? He was never going to know if he didn't ask her for a real date, but he wasn't going to ask tonight. Maybe on Saturday when he had dinner at her house. He was working up to this slowly. First a dance, then a date.

When the last note faded, Melanie looked up at him. "Thanks so much for asking me to dance. I'm so glad I didn't step on your toes."

"And here I was worried about stepping on *your* toes." Relief washing over him, Nathan laughed, his tension fading.

Melanie joined his laughter as the disc jockey started another fast song. "That's too funny. We were both worried about the same thing. Tim used to tell me I liked to lead."

Nathan didn't know how to respond to Melanie's comment about Tim, but it served to remind Nathan that he didn't have first place in her thoughts. Had she been thinking about Tim the whole time they'd been dancing? Nathan realized he wasn't only battling his own doubts. He was battling Melanie's memories, too.

How was he going to deal with those? She was never going to forget Tim, especially with her boys. Then Nathan realized how selfish his thoughts were. This was the anniversary of the day she'd met Tim. Of course, Tim was going to be at the forefront of her thoughts tonight, and this wedding could've been a heartrending experience. She'd mentioned how the ceremony might bring some tears. Nathan was glad that her memories at this moment appeared to make her happy rather than sad.

Nathan wondered how he could possibly fit into her life when Tim's memory held her heart. "If you want to lead, that's fine with me. I'm not much for the fast dancing. I guess you can join the other women. You all seem to enjoy it."

"Yeah, it's been fun, but I think I'll take a little breather. So I'm going back to my table to sit down."

Nathan decided he was through being a coward. "Come sit at my table."

"But isn't your table full of the folks who were assigned to sit there?"

"It was, but people have moved around and are sitting anywhere now that dinner is over. If we have to, we can always pull up one more chair."

"Okay." Her face radiated with joy. "I'd better retrieve my purse from the other table."

Her expression made Nathan's pulse race as if he'd just finished dancing to one of those fast songs.

While he stood there watching Melanie, Juliane appeared at his side. "That looked like it went pretty well, didn't it?"

"What?"

"Your dance with Melanie." Juliane grinned at him.

Nathan held Juliane's gaze. "Yes, it did."

"Are there more dances in your future?"

"No."

"Come on. You two looked good together."

"Maybe we did, but we're not going to dance again. We're going to sit and talk for a while and get to know each other better. And I can't do that while I'm dancing. I have to concentrate too much on my feet to talk." Nathan chuckled and glanced in the direction of Melanie's table. "Excuse me. Here she comes."

"So you've had a change of heart?"

"No, I'm doing this just to get you to quit bugging me." Nathan didn't turn around to look at Juliane's expression, but he was pretty sure she was standing there with her mouth open. He met Melanie halfway. "Got your purse?"

She held up a tiny navy-blue bag with shiny beads all over it. They matched the beading on the little jacket she wore over her navy and white dress that hung several inches below her knees. She suddenly looked ill at ease. "Where do we sit?"

"You look very nice tonight."

"Thanks." She held out the sides of her skirt. "You mean you like this better than my scrubs with the dancing toothbrushes?"

"I like the scrubs, too, but you look especially good in this dress."

"You're too kind."

"No, just being honest."

"Well, thank you again. I don't get many chances to get dressed up." She shrugged. "But then people don't dress up very much anymore."

"Yeah. That's what my mother says. She remembers the days when the women wore dresses and hats to church."

"Now you see all kinds of clothes, but I don't think that's entirely a bad thing, do you?"

"Don't ask me to comment on fashion, but I do have to say it's nice not to have to wear a tie on Sundays anymore." Nathan laughed as they reached the table where he'd been sitting.

"But I've seen you in a suit and tie at church."

Pleased that Melanie had noticed, Nathan pulled out a chair for her at what was now an empty table, which Nathan didn't mind at all. "Yeah, but it was my choice.

"I can't imagine trying to get Ryan and Andrew to wear a tie to church. I'm pretty sure they associate wearing a tie with Tim's funeral." Pressing her lips together, Melanie lowered her head.

Nathan wondered whether she was trying to keep herself from crying. She had seemed so happy up until this point, even when she'd been talking about Tim. Should he say anything— try to comfort her? Anything he tried to say would probably be inadequate.

Looking up, she put on a brave face as a forced smile curved her mouth—that very kissable mouth. Here she was feeling sad about the loss of her husband, but all Nathan could think about was kissing her again. He rubbed the back of his neck and looked away. How bad was he? He didn't want to answer his own question.

As Nathan stared at the floor, he felt the touch of Melanie's hand on his. "I'm sorry. I've been talking about Tim way too much tonight."

Knitting his eyebrows, Nathan glanced up. "No. No you haven't. He has to be on your mind since it's the anniversary of the day you met Tim. It's only natural that you'd think about him and talk about him."

"Thank you for understanding." She smiled again—a genuine, unforced smile.

"You're welcome. Like I told you before, I can't begin to understand what you went through." Nathan liked seeing her smile return.

"And thanks again for taking the boys and me to the baseball game. They haven't stopped talking about it." Melanie laughed. "Ryan keeps looking at the foul ball he caught like it's some expensive treasure. I'm so afraid he's going to take it out to show his friends and lose it."

"Maybe you could get some kind of trophy case to put it in—one that he can't open."

Melanie frowned. "Do they make such a thing?"

"I don't know, but my mom's cousin owns a trophy shop, and he orders the uniforms for the youth baseball teams, so I could ask him if you'd like."

"That would be wonderful." Melanie clasped her hands together.

"I'll check into it. Remind me if I forget."

"I'll tell Ryan, and he won't let you forget." Melanie laughed again.

"You're right." Hoping he was at least a little part of her happiness at the moment, Nathan joined her laughter. "Who's watching Ryan and Andrew tonight?"

"The teenage girl down the street." Melanie grimaced. "I hope the boys don't give her a hard time. Sometimes, they can be a handful."

Shaking his head, Nathan chuckled. "I can remember when my brother and I used to torment the babysitters."

"You mean you were a rascally little boy?"

"I was."

"But you turned out okay."

Nathan smiled. "Thanks for the vote of confidence. That's good to hear."

Melanie glanced at her watch. "I can't stay much longer. I told the babysitter that I'd be home by eleven-thirty."

"Then you've got time for one more dance." Nathan glanced at the dance floor where Juliane actually had Lukas dancing to an old rock-and-roll song, along with Seth and Elise.

"You mean you're going to let me lead."

"If you'd like." Nathan couldn't help smiling. "And I promise not to step on your toes."

Melanie's laughter mixed with the final notes of the lively song.

"Okay if we dance to the next slow song?"

"As long as they play it before I have to leave."

"You have a request?"

Melanie shook her head. "I can never think of the names of songs to make a request."

"Me neither." Nathan stood. "I'll go ask the disc jockey to play something slow—his choice."

"That sounds good." Melanie smiled up at him.

As the next spirited song came over the speakers, Nathan talked with the disc jockey. As he returned to the table, he thought about asking her to dance now, even to a fast song, but he didn't want her to see that he had absolutely no rhythm. He hoped she could stay for the slow one.

Sitting, he looked at Melanie. "He says he has a slow number programmed to play after the next two songs. Can you stay until he plays it?"

Melanie looked at her watch again. "That could be cutting it close."

Nathan could see the indecision in her eyes. He wanted to tell her to call the sitter and say she'd be a little late, but that was selfish thinking—something he seemed to be doing a lot of tonight. "That's okay. We'll dance at the next wedding."

Whoa. He was getting way ahead of himself.

"I suppose that might be Dot and Ferd."

"You mean Lukas's grandfather?"

"Yeah. You didn't know? Where have you been?"

The question hit him right where he lived. He'd focused his attention on the bank and hadn't been paying attention to the things going on around him, especially Melanie. More than two years had passed since she'd become a widow, and he was just now noticing her. He could've been getting to know her during that time. But even after two years, was she ready to have an interest in another man? He hoped he wasn't pushing her with his attention. That's one reason he wanted to take things slowly. He had to gauge where she was in life.

The next song started, and Melanie picked up her little purse and plucked out her cell phone. "I'd hate to miss that dance. I'll give my sitter a call and tell her I might be a few minutes late."

"Okay." Nathan's heart sang. She was doing exactly what he'd wished she'd do. She was willing to stay a little longer so she could dance one more time with him. But he cautioned himself not to read anything into it. Maybe she just enjoyed dancing.

Melanie spent a minute talking to her sitter, then ended the call. Slipping the phone into her purse, she looked at him. "We're good to go."

"Thanks. I appreciate your giving me one more chance to step on your toes."

Melanie laughed. "Next time I'll wear my steel-toed shoes."

"You have a pair?"

"Yeah, actually I do. Tim made me buy some when we were using pavers to construct a backyard patio for our first house."

"You did your own patio? And with pavers? That's a lot of work." Raising his eyebrows, Nathan wondered whether he'd ever be able to compete with Tim's memory. He seemed to have been able to do anything.

"Yeah, Tim liked to do that kind of stuff. He sat behind a desk all week, so he enjoyed working with his hands on the weekends." Melanie shook her head. "I'm sorry. Here I am going on and on about Tim again."

"You can talk about him as much as you'd like." Nathan figured he'd have to get used to hearing about Tim if he was going to get to know Melanie.

"You're too nice—and so understanding."

"Don't go telling anyone that. You'll ruin my image."

"And what is your image?"

"The hard-nosed banker?"

"Maybe the nose-to-the-grindstone banker."

"Oh, so you've been talking to Juliane? That's the way she describes me."

Melanie shook her head. "Juliane's never said anything to me about that. I've just observed that you're a very busy man."

Forcing a laugh, Nathan knew her assessment was right, but, on the brighter side, she'd noticed. As he wondered which was better, the beginning strains of a ballad sung by Kenny Rogers started. Nathan held out his hand. "This is it."

Melanie placed her hand in his as he led her to the dance floor. This time he didn't worry about having to talk to her or stepping on her toes. He just appreciated holding her in his arms as they moved to the music. He was beginning to believe that she enjoyed being with him. Once again the words to the song went right to the heart of his growing feelings for this woman. She'd stepped into his life and colored his world.

When the song ended, she gazed up at him. "Thank you for a very nice ending to my evening."

"It was definitely my pleasure." Nathan still held her hand as they left the dance floor. "Let me walk you to your car."

"Okay. Thanks. I'll grab my purse, then say goodbye to Seth and Elise."

After she returned, he led the way to the entrance and opened the door. They stepped out into the cool night air. A full moon shone overhead while crickets chirped in stereo.

Nathan glanced at Melanie, her face bathed in moonlight. "Where's your car?"

"Right under the security light about halfway down this middle row." Melanie pointed straight ahead. "Tim always taught me to park near a light."

"Good advice."

Melanie put a hand to her mouth, then grimaced. "I'm so sorry. I did it again."

"Don't worry about it."

"You are—"

Nathan held up his hand. "Don't say it. If you keep praising me, I'll get a big head."

"I doubt it."

Nathan was about to protest again when he noticed that one of the back tires on Melanie's car didn't look quite right. He leaned over to examine it more closely. "You've got a flat tire."

"How could that be? Everything was fine when I drove here."

"You could've picked up a nail somewhere between your house and here, and the air slowly leaked out." Nathan shrugged. "You never know."

Melanie dug in her purse and produced her cell phone. "Guess I'll have to call the auto club and then the sitter. What a way to ruin a good evening."

Nathan reached over and touched her arm. "You don't need to call the auto club. You'd have to wait for them. Then you'd get home even later than you intended. I'll take you home. My cousin Mike, who owns the tire store out on the highway, is here tonight. I'll get him to take care of it."

"You're a lifesaver. Thanks."

Nathan motioned toward some parking places at the side of the building. "My car's over here."

As Nathan made the five-minute trip to Melanie's house,

she called her sitter to let her know she was on the way home. After Nathan pulled into her driveway, he quickly went around to the other side of his SUV to help her out. "I'm going to give my cousin a call on my cell right now, and I'll let you know what the plan is."

"Thanks." Melanie disappeared into the house.

As Nathan finished talking with his cousin, Melanie reappeared with the sitter, who started walking down the street. "Does she need a ride home?"

Walking toward him, Melanie shook her head. "She lives two doors down. I always wait on the driveway and watch until she goes into her house."

"Good." Nathan pocketed his phone.

Melanie waved as the sitter opened her front door and went inside, then turned to Nathan. "What did you find out?"

"Mike said he'd get your tire fixed early tomorrow morning. So you'll have your car back in time to drive to church. If he can't repair the tire, he'll put on a new one." Nathan held out his hand. "If you'll give me your car keys, I'll take them to him when I go back to the reception."

"That sounds like a good plan. My keys are in my purse. It'll take me just seconds to get them."

"I'll wait right here." Watching her go into the house, Nathan was happy that he could help her.

When she returned, she held out the keys to him. Their fingers touched as he took them, and Nathan couldn't ignore his reaction. Pulse racing. Stomach churning. Nerves zinging. He didn't want to wait to ask her for that date, but he wished he knew how she'd respond. "I'd offer to pick you and the boys up for church in the morning, but I'm meeting my dad for breakfast. Bank business."

Melanie put a hand over her heart. "That wouldn't be necessary. You've done enough already."

Moonlight bathed Melanie's lovely face as they stood on

the front walk near the driveway. When she looked up at him with those big dark eyes, he could hardly keep himself from taking her in his arms and kissing her. He should ask her for a date now. A lump crowded his throat. He swallowed hard. "Do you like going to movies?"

"Yes, if they're a good ones. T—" Melanie dropped her gaze.

Nathan knew she'd been about to say something about Tim, but had stopped herself. Was that a good thing? Nathan wished he knew. He didn't want to make life harder for her. Maybe he shouldn't ask her for a date, after all but he wasn't going to let second thoughts win. "Tonight during dinner, Elise and Juliane were telling me about this movie that's coming to town in a couple of weeks that's supposed to be a good one. It's a romantic comedy."

Melanie smiled. "Probably one you guys aren't very interested in seeing."

"Probably not, but I'd like to take you anyway. Would you like to go a week from Saturday?" A huge lump formed in Nathan's throat as he waited for her answer.

A little frown puckered Melanie's brow. "Are you asking me for a date?"

Nathan tried to laugh. "Clumsily, but yes I am."

"I accept. I'd love to go."

"Super. Then it's a date."

"It is."

As Nathan drove back to the reception, he couldn't help thinking about their last dance and the words of Kenny Rogers's song. Melanie was definitely decorating his life—making it better than ever before. But his thinking had been one-sided tonight. He was thinking only about his wants and not hers. Could he decorate her world, or would he only complicate it?

Chapter Ten

On the Monday evening following Elise and Seth's wedding, Melanie scooted into the bleachers next to Juliane. "Thanks for saving me a seat, even though we're on opposite sides tonight."

Juliane laughed. "Yeah. I'm sorry, but I'm going to have to cheer against your boys' team."

With the crowd noise buzzing around her, Melanie glanced at the ball field, but she didn't see Nathan. His assistant was talking to the kids. Did she dare ask about Nathan, or would her question raise Juliane's curiosity? Melanie wasn't sure whether Nathan had mentioned their upcoming date. If he hadn't, she certainly didn't want to tell Juliane. "Well, I won't hold it against you."

"That's good to hear."

"Have you heard from Elise and Seth?"

"Yeah, they called Mom and Dad's to talk to Olivia and wish Dad a happy Father's Day. They are having a fabulous time in Colorado. Elise says the mountains are beautiful."

"How is Olivia doing without her daddy?"

"She's doing fine. She's really too little to understand much about Father's Day, so that wasn't an issue. And my mom is having the time of her life watching Olivia."

"That's wonderful." While Melanie watched her boys taking a little fielding practice before the start of the game, she thought of the emptiness that accompanied Father's Day since Tim's death. She always let the boys call and talk to their grandfather, but for her there was no joy in the day.

The coaches were meeting with the umpires, but Nathan still wasn't there. Ever since the night of Elise and Seth's wedding, Melanie had been waiting to be with Nathan again. She'd seen him slip in and out of church on Sunday, but he was gone before she could even say hello. She knew he was extra busy at the bank, but after he'd asked her for a date, she couldn't stop thinking about him.

Melanie turned back to Juliane. "Looks like they're about ready to start."

"You're right." Juliane frowned. "Where's Nathan? I don't see him. Have you?"

Shaking her head, Melanie wondered whether she should admit that she'd been looking for him, too. Then she saw him racing from the parking lot toward his team's bench. A sense of well-being settled over her. "There he is."

Juliane sighed. "He was probably working late at the bank again. He needs to quit burning the candle at both ends."

Melanie wanted to defend Nathan, but she imagined that would prompt Juliane to ask all kinds of questions that Melanie couldn't answer. She wanted time for Nathan and her to figure out where things were going with them before she let other people know about their involvement. Her boys didn't even know that Nathan had asked her for a date. She thought she would tell them when Nathan came for supper on Saturday.

"Well, I know my boys are glad to see him. They think he can do no wrong."

"And what about you?"

"I think he's a pretty good coach. My boys seem to be

learning a lot, and they are thrilled to be playing baseball. I'm so glad Nathan thought to ask about them playing."

Juliane poked Melanie. "You're avoiding my question."

"No, I'm not. I told you I think he's a good coach."

"That's not what I meant, and you know it."

Hoping to ward off Juliane's inquisition, Melanie frowned. "You're beginning to repeat yourself a lot."

Juliane chuckled. "Okay. I don't want to know why your face lit up when you saw Nathan."

"Good. Then we won't have to talk about it." Melanie gave Juliane a cheesy grin. "Let's watch the game."

"Are you going to the Dairy Barn after the game?"

"Yeah, we'll have to celebrate our victory."

"Don't get too confident."

Melanie eyed Juliane. "Losers buy ice cream?"

"Deal." Juliane gave Melanie a high five.

The young ball players displayed moments of proficient skill mixed with errors and missteps. The adults and big brothers and sisters cheered on their teams, clapping and yelling when their favorite player came to bat or made a catch or a throw for an out. Melanie beamed with pride when Ryan hit a double into the outfield and batted in one of his teammates for a run. The next two batters were thrown out at first base, so Ryan didn't get to score.

Besides being delighted with the way Ryan and Andrew were playing, Melanie noticed the way Nathan praised the children on his team. He never raised his voice, even when they messed up. He helped them by reminding them how to use proper form when batting or fielding a ball.

In the bottom of the last inning, Nathan's team had the lead by one run. There were two outs, and Lukas's team had a runner at second base.

Juliane glanced Melanie's way. "Well, this is it. We have to score here, or it looks like I'll be buying you ice cream."

Melanie cupped her hands around her mouth. "Strike him out!"

Melanie heard the ping of the metal bat as the little boy on Lukas's team connected with the pitch. Her heart jumped into her throat as she watched the ball sail into right field, headed toward Andrew. He stuck his glove in the air. Melanie didn't know whether she could watch. If he didn't catch the ball the other team would win. Holding her breath, she was tempted to close her eyes, but she watched and hoped. The cheers and clapping seemed far away, and everything seemed to move in slow motion as the ball moved through the air toward Andrew.

Then in an instant the ball landed in Andrew's glove. He closed his other hand over it to keep it from falling out. Melanie began jumping up and down and cheering at the top of her lungs. The kids from Andrew's team who were still on the bench raced onto the field, joining their teammates as they crowded around Andrew.

A lump rose in her throat and tears welled in her eyes. Her baby had caught the ball. While she stood there absorbing what had happened, she realized that the other parents were going onto the field to congratulate their children.

Juliane pulled on one of Melanie's arms. "Come on. You have to congratulate your boys. I'll congratulate them, too, even though they beat Lukas's team. And I guess that means I have to buy ice cream."

"Okay. Let's go." Melanie took the bleacher steps two at a time.

When they reached the field, Andrew ran up to her. "Mom, did you see me catch the ball? I closed my glove and put my other hand over it like Coach taught me."

"Good job." Wishing she could hug him, Melanie patted his head instead. She didn't want to embarrass him, so she'd save the hugs for home.

While the jubilant clamor sounded around her, Ryan sprinted over and tugged on her arm. "Did you see my double?"

"I did. You really connected with that ball. Both you and your brother played very well tonight, and you helped your team win."

When the hubbub died down, the coaches gathered the teams to shake hands. Nathan looked her way and smiled. Her heart did a little dance. Melanie couldn't believe how good it felt to see him smiling at her. She was thrilled and worried all at the same time. She wanted what was best for her boys. Was a new relationship with Nathan going to be a good thing? She thought so, but that was something she would have to find out.

After the teams finished shaking hands, Nathan and Lukas joined Melanie and Juliane. Lukas gave Juliane a hug, and Melanie wished Nathan could do the same to her. The thought surprised her. They hadn't had their first date, and he was already winning her heart.

Nathan gave her a wry smile. "You got a little excited tonight. I could hear you all the way down on the field."

Melanie felt herself blush. "I was just cheering for my boys."

"That's the way to go, Mom." Nathan patted her on the back.

"Quit teasing me." Not really minding that he teased her, Melanie knew that her face was getting redder by the minute. "Are you joining us at the Dairy Barn tonight?"

Juliane waved a hand in the air. "Yeah, I'm buying, since Lukas's team lost."

"Well, since you're buying, I'll have to go," Nathan said.

"Yay!" Ryan and Andrew jumped up and down.

"Okay, I'll have to console my husband. We'll see you in a few minutes at the Dairy Barn." Heading toward the parking lot, Juliane looped an arm through Lukas's.

As Juliane and Lukas left, Melanie ushered her boys toward her car. Nathan fell into step beside them. "Mike tells me he was able to fix your tire and didn't have to replace it."

"Yeah. That was a relief. A lot cheaper than a new tire. I'm so glad you noticed before I drove away."

"I'm glad I was there to see it, too, or you probably would've had to get a new one." Nathan stopped beside his car, which parked two spaces down from Melanie's. "I'll meet you at the Dairy Barn."

Andrew danced around in front of Melanie. "Mom, can we ride with Coach?"

Melanie glanced down at her excited youngster. "Sweetie, he doesn't have your booster seats in his car."

Andrew's shoulders sagged. "Okay. We'll ride with you."

Melanie pressed her lips together to keep from smiling as she looked over the boys' heads at Nathan. "I'm so sorry you're stuck with your mom. I think you can live without Coach for the five minutes it takes to get to the Dairy Barn. What do you think?"

"Yeah." Andrew pouted.

Melanie punched the unlock button on her remote. "Go get into the car, and I'll be there in a minute. I need to talk to Coach."

"You sound so serious. Did I do something wrong?" Nathan stared at her.

"No, I wanted to tell you I haven't told the boys that we're going on a date."

"Are you changing your mind?"

"Oh, no." Melanie sighed. "I'm just not sure how to bring it up or how they'll react. They think you're the best, but I don't know… How do I explain it?"

Nodding, Nathan touched her arm. "Are you worried that they'll think you're trying to replace their father?"

Melanie shrugged. "I'm not sure that's it, either."

"What do you think about my asking for their permission to take you out?"

"What if they say no?" Melanie looked at him, her dark eyes wide.

"Do you think that's going to happen?"

Shaking her head, Melanie chuckled. "Probably not. I think they'll be excited, but I wasn't sure. So I've been stewing about it since you asked. But I like your idea."

"Okay, I'll ask when I come to supper on Saturday."

"Thanks." Melanie squeezed his hand. "I knew you'd know what to do. See you in a few minutes."

As Melanie drove to the Dairy Barn, she realized how Nathan had become so much a part of her thoughts and her life. Was that good? She shouldn't be worried. She'd already accepted a date with him. That should mean she'd set her worries aside. She trusted Nathan, but the fear of what Tim's parents would say still niggled at the back of her mind. Maybe that's why she hadn't told the boys. She was afraid they would tell Harlan and Georgia Drake. Melanie had to stop letting the Drakes intimidate her. Having Nathan in their lives *was* a good thing, so she needed to be brave and deal with the difficulties.

Children's squeals and laughter filled the night air as Nathan walked across the parking lot at the Dairy Barn. His mind was still cluttered with details concerning the ongoing bank audit, but he wanted to be here with Melanie and her boys. The bank was beginning to find second place in his life. He wasn't sure whether that was good or bad.

His title at the bank hadn't changed, but essentially he was in charge. Anything that went wrong was on his shoulders. The stress had been building in the past couple of weeks with the ongoing audit that consumed his thoughts. During their last audit, the bank had received an excellent rating, so he wanted to do as well this time. Since their compliance officer had been out for the past six months with a difficult pregnancy, others had tried to step in to fill the gap, but he still feared that her absence would result in some problems.

Stress was a trigger for his Crohn's, and here he was worrying about worrying. None of this could be good.

Even Ryan and Andrew's excited greeting didn't completely do away with his anxiety. They each grabbed a hand and nearly dragged him to the table where Melanie sat.

Lukas saluted as Nathan took a seat at the picnic table next to Melanie. "To the victors go the spoils. Juliane and I are taking orders."

Nathan held out a hand toward Melanie. "Ladies first."

"Chocolate and vanilla swirl." Juliane glanced at the boys. "What about you guys?"

"Chocolate and vanilla swirl," they said in unison.

"Me, too." Nathan looked over at Lukas. "Would you like me to help you carry something?"

Lukas waved a hand as if he were stopping traffic. "No need. Juliane and I will take care of everything."

"Okay." Nathan detected a conspiratorial glance between Lukas and Juliane. He figured they were still trying to push Melanie and him together. Little did they know there was no conspiracy needed.

While Lukas and Juliane got the ice cream cones, Nathan listened with amusement as Ryan and Andrew did nearly a play-by-play rehash of their game with special emphasis on their starring roles.

Andrew's expression brightened. "Mom, can we call Grandma and Grandpa to tell them about our game?"

Nathan saw Melanie's hesitation. How could those people make this lovely woman worry about her kids calling them?

"Okay." Melanie fished her cell phone from her purse,

then punched in the number. "Here you go. Take turns and be polite."

While the boys took turns talking on the phone, Nathan heard the elation in their voices, and he saw the expression on Melanie's face. She almost appeared to be holding her breath, as if she was worried that the boys would make some kind of miscue. Nathan wondered what was coming from the other end of the conversation. What kind of people made Melanie look as though she were sitting on pins and needles even when she wasn't talking to them?

After the little boys ended their conversation and returned the phone to Melanie, they volunteered little about the call. Before Nathan could ask a question about it, Juliane and Lukas reappeared with the ice cream cones. Nathan regretted his unkind thoughts about the people he'd never met and decided not to dwell on them. Maybe Juliane and Lukas's arrival had saved him from butting in where he didn't belong.

While Nathan enjoyed the ice cream, along with the others, he tried to push thoughts about the bank audit and the Drakes from his mind and just concentrate on the camaraderie around him. He let Ryan and Andrew's laughter wrap around his heart and give him peace. Something about being with these kids made him less apt to think about his own troubles.

"You're awfully quiet tonight." Juliane looked at him as she finished her ice cream cone.

"I'm too busy enjoying my ice cream to talk." After Melanie had talked to him, Nathan didn't want to give even the slightest hint that they had a date planned. He didn't want to accidentally say something. So keeping quiet was his best option.

"Hey, Mom. Can we go play with the other kids over there?" Ryan pointed toward the playground.

Melanie nodded. "Okay, but stay where I can see you."

"We will." Ryan and Andrew dashed off before their mother had a chance to say another word.

"Even a baseball game doesn't seem to diminish their energy." Melanie sighed. "Sometimes, I wish I could bottle it."

"I think they do. Don't they call them energy drinks?" Juliane laughed.

Everyone around the table chuckled. As their talk turned to the upcoming Fourth of July festivities in Kellerville, Nathan could see Melanie's earlier tension drain from her shoulders. She may have lost her anxiety, but Nathan gained it when Juliane tried to talk him into singing on the church float. He was taking time out to coach youth baseball, but he didn't have extra time for singing. But sometimes trying to convince Juliane was an impossible task.

Nathan knew, despite his dad's seemingly happy-go-lucky attitude of late about the goings-on at the bank, that if anything went wrong with the audit, his dad wouldn't be easy to live with. Nathan would have to shoulder the responsibility, but he would handle whatever came his way. Irritated that he'd let bank business occupy his thoughts again, Nathan gave himself a mental shake. Before he could focus his mind on something else, a loud cry came from the playground area.

Ryan came running up to the table, his eyes wide. "Mom, come quick. Andrew's hurt."

Melanie jumped up from the table and raced after Ryan. Nathan followed. They met Andrew who had a gash on his forehead and blood dripping down his face and onto his shirt. Bawling, he ran into Melanie's arms. She gathered him close, not caring that now her clothes were bloody, too. "What happened?"

Worry wrinkled Ryan's little brow. "He tripped and fell while we were chasing each other. Is he going to be all right?"

Nathan pulled a handkerchief from his pocket. "This is clean. Let me put it on the cut to stop the blood."

Melanie didn't speak, merely nodded, as Andrew continued to cry.

Juliane and Lukas hovered nearby. Juliane stepped closer. "Is there anything we can do?"

Pressing the handkerchief to Andrew's head, Nathan looked first at Juliane, than at Melanie's ashen face. "There's nothing you or Lukas can do. I think we should take him to the emergency room. That cut looks like it'll need stitches."

"Okay." Melanie's voice barely sounded above Andrew's crying.

Sensing that he needed to take charge, Nathan hunkered down beside Melanie and Andrew. "I'll carry him to the car. You go ahead and unlock it. You can sit with him in the back, and I'll drive to the hospital."

Melanie nodded. After releasing Andrew to Nathan's arms, she grabbed Ryan's hand and sprinted to her car. She unlocked it and opened the back door. "Ryan, get yourself buckled in."

"Let us know if there's anything we can do to help," Juliane called to Nathan.

"Will do." Nathan deposited Andrew in his booster seat and helped Melanie get him settled in. She seemed much calmer, despite the way her hand trembled as she handed Nathan her keys. She continued to hold the handkerchief to Andrew's head. His cries subsided, as they made the ten-minute drive to the hospital. When they arrived, Melanie wanted to carry Andrew into the emergency room, but the boy insisted on walking. Hopefully, that was a good indication that nothing was seriously wrong.

They signed in at the registration desk, and a minute later a triage nurse came out and talked to them. Thankfully, the emergency room was relatively quiet and their wait for an exam room wasn't long. Melanie reassured Ryan that Andrew was going to be okay, and Nathan sensed that she was reassuring herself, as well. He didn't miss the way she tried to hide her own reaction to being in the emergency room. Nathan figured she was probably remembering the night Tim was brought here and didn't recover.

Over the years, Nathan had become familiar with this emergency room. He remembered the time he'd also gotten stitches and another time when he'd broken his leg in middle school. Then there was the time in high school when he'd dislocated his shoulder while playing football. Even the time he'd come in because he'd been dehydrated, before they figured out he had Crohn's disease, hadn't been a life-or-death situation. And he hadn't been here when Seth had been brought in after his horrific car accident. So Nathan couldn't imagine the trauma.

When the nurse called Andrew back, Melanie went with him. Nathan remained in the waiting area with Ryan. The little boy looked through some battered books that sat on a nearby table, then looked up at Nathan. "I don't like emergency rooms. They have terrible books."

"You're right." Nathan knew Ryan's dislike of emergency rooms had nothing to do with the books, but everything to do with the night his father had died. Returning had to be upsetting for all of them.

Nathan tried to be as comforting as possible as he and Ryan waited. As Nathan sat there, he realized he hadn't bothered to pray in a long time. He'd let his busy life get in the way, and he wasn't sure how he was going to change that. He didn't want prayer to be just one more thing he had to put on his to-do list. Would God help him if he prayed about praying? Would talking to God help him figure out how to deal with his growing feelings for Melanie? Nathan wasn't sure. But one thing he could do now—pray with Ryan.

Nathan touched Ryan's arm. "Would you like to pray for Andrew?"

Wide-eyed, Ryan nodded, then bowed his head. "Dear God, please help Andrew's head to be okay. Thank You. Amen." Then Ryan looked up. "You gonna pray, too?"

"Yes." Nathan bowed his head. "Thank You, Lord, that You hear our prayers. Thank You that Andrew has a big brother who cares about him. We ask You to be with Andrew and ask that his head will heal quickly. In Jesus's name we pray. Amen."

"Thank you for praying." Ryan's expression beamed with sincerity and a hint of relief.

"You're welcome. Thanks for asking me." Nathan couldn't help thinking how much this time with Ryan had brought them closer. Nathan could see that, although the brothers sometimes didn't get along, Ryan really cared about his little brother.

Moments later, Melanie and Andrew returned to the waiting area. Andrew was all smiles, and Melanie appeared relieved that it was all over.

"Look at my stitches. Cool, huh?" Andrew stuck his head forward.

Melanie shook her head. "Such a badge of honor."

"Good to see you smiling. I'm glad they could put you back together." Nathan patted Andrew on the back.

"Does this mean you can't play baseball?" Ryan asked.

Melanie nodded. "Probably not this week. He'll have to wait until the stitches come out in about a week."

"Is he going to have a scar like a gangster?" Ryan studied the six stitches that formed what looked like a little railroad track on Andrew's forehead just below his hairline.

"No, the scar will probably look a lot like this." Nathan lifted his chin and pointed to a place just under his jaw line. "I've got you beat, Andrew. Fourteen stitches."

After Andrew and Ryan examined Nathan's scar, Andrew gazed up at Nathan. "That's a super-cool scar!"

"Were you in a fight?" Ryan asked.

"No. I—"

"How *did* you get it?" Despite her question, Melanie didn't seem nearly as impressed or amused.

Nathan put an arm around Melanie's shoulders. "I didn't mean to make light of Andrew's injury."

"That's okay. How did you got that scar?"

"My brother and I were climbing a tree, and I fell and hit a sharp rock. I was stitched up right here just like Andrew."

"Remind me not to let my boys climb trees."

"Ah, Mom." Ryan frowned. "We won't be clumsy like Nathan."

Nathan laughed. "That puts me in my place."

As they left the emergency room, Ryan and Andrew walked ahead. Nathan fell into step with Melanie. "Are you doing okay?"

Nodding, she gave him that uncertain smile that always seemed to turn him inside out. "Now that it's all over, I'm all right, but I don't want to go through that again."

"I hate to tell you this, but I believe you'll probably find yourself in this emergency room a few more times before your boys are grown." Nathan pointed to his chin. "This was only one of numerous trips I took here."

Melanie stopped and looked up at him. She reached out and touched the scar. "That must've given your mom a real scare."

"It did." With her standing so close, Nathan couldn't think straight. He took a deep breath in order to collect his thoughts. "Well, we'd better drive over to get my car and let you get home."

"Thanks for everything. I don't know what I would've done without you tonight."

"Any time you need me, I'll be there." He'd told her that before, but it was true now more than ever. He couldn't forget what Melanie had said the day of his grandmother's birthday party. She was thankful that Lukas and Nathan were part of her boys' lives. He had to put aside any personal worries and make sure he helped these little boys have a good life.

While he drove back to the Dairy Barn, he replayed the evening in his mind. Once again Nathan knew this was a taste of family life—the good and the bad. He longed for it more than ever.

Chapter Eleven

The doorbell rang. Ryan and Andrew raced from the kitchen toward the front door.

"I got it," Andrew yelled.

Ryan chased after Andrew. "No, I got it."

As Melanie stepped into the front hall, they were fighting over who would get to open the door. Ryan pushed Andrew aside and tried to grab the doorknob.

"Stop that right now. You could tear open Andrew's stitches." Melanie glared at them as they turned and stared at her. "While you boys are fighting, Nathan is standing out there wondering why no one has answered the door."

Ryan pointed at Andrew. "He started it."

"I don't want to hear about it." She lined them up against the wall. "Stand here and be quiet while I answer the door."

Turning the knob, Melanie prayed that nothing else would go wrong. She didn't need the boys fighting on top of having to deal with Tim's parents. During the Drakes' weekly phone call with the boys, Andrew had bragged about his emergency-room visit, and Melanie had had to deal with all their questions about his accident. She'd been waiting to see Nathan all day, and she didn't want anything to ruin their evening.

Taking a deep breath, she opened the door. Her heart

melted when she saw him grinning that lopsided grin. "Hi, come in."

"Hi. It's good to see you." Nathan stepped inside and handed her a bouquet of pink peonies.

"Thank you. These are beautiful." Melanie brought the flowers to her nose. "Oh, they smell good, too. Sorry it took so long for me to open the door."

"Did I hear a little—"

"Oh, no. You heard them arguing." How long would a man be interested in a woman with two unruly kids? She had to hope the rest of the evening went better than the beginning.

"No, I just heard some kids eager to see me." Nathan glanced at Ryan and Andrew, who stood like statues against the wall. "Right, guys?"

With their little backs still plastered to the wall, they nodded their heads.

Breathing deeply, Nathan looked back at Melanie. "That manicotti sure smells good. My taste buds have been thinking about it all day."

"Taste buds don't think." Andrew laughed, but didn't move an inch off the wall.

"Mine do." Nathan winked.

Ryan hunched his shoulders. "Mom, can we get off the wall now?"

"You may go as long as you walk calmly back to the kitchen. No running. No yelling."

The boys cautiously pushed themselves away from the wall. Their stiff movement down the hall told Melanie that they could barely keep themselves from racing each other again.

Nathan leaned over and whispered, "How are things going with Andrew?"

"Pretty good, but I'll be glad when the stitches come out on Tuesday. I keep thinking he's going to do something and tear them open. Like tonight—tussling to open the front door."

"I hear that Ryan hit a home run during Wednesday's game." Nathan sighed. "Sorry I wasn't there to see it, but dad and I were going over the bank examiners' report."

"How's that going?"

"It's going. That's about all I can say. I'll be glad when we've had our meeting and it's all over, because it's consumed too much of my thinking."

"Coach, see what Mom got for us." Ryan tugged on Nathan's arm and pointed at the fireplace mantel. "She even let us keep it up here instead of in the basement."

Nathan saw two baseballs enclosed in a clear plastic case. "Is one of those the foul ball you caught?"

Standing up tall, Ryan gazed at the case. "Yeah, and the other one's my home run ball."

"That's nice. Your mom did a good job for you."

Melanie went to the kitchen and found a vase. After filling it with water, she arranged the peonies in it and set it on the counter. Then she got a loaf of garlic bread out of the oven. The smell of garlic wafted through the air as she placed it in a small wicker basket. "You guys can go to the table."

"Can I help with something?"

Melanie shook her head. "No. The manicotti and the salad are already on the table. Oh, I made some zucchini for you since you don't do salads."

"Thanks." Nathan took a seat, but he looked uncertain when she'd mentioned the zucchini.

Wondering whether Nathan didn't like vegetables, Melanie brought the bread to the table and sat down. After a prayer, they began to eat. The boys talked and laughed with no sign of their earlier disagreement. They badgered Nathan with questions about his job at the bank, about baseball and about half a dozen other subjects. He answered them all, taking special care to make sure they understood. His patience with her boys warmed her heart.

As the meal progressed, Melanie kept wondering whether Nathan remembered how he intended to talk to the boys about their date. Had he forgotten about his plan? Or maybe he'd forgotten about the date. Perhaps he didn't even want to go on the date anymore.

When Nathan finished his meal, he gave her that lopsided grin. "Your manicotti's even better than your spaghetti."

"There's more if you'd like some."

He patted his stomach. "I've already had two servings. I'd better not overdo it."

"Let me send some home with you."

"I'll take you up on that."

"Mom, after you clean up, can we play a game?" Andrew picked up his plate and headed for the kitchen. "I'll help you load the dishwasher."

Melanie couldn't believe Andrew was volunteering to clean up. She usually had to cajole the boys to help with the cleanup after meals. "Thanks. I can always use your help."

Standing, Nathan grabbed his plate. "Since your mom did the cooking, she should sit down and relax while we men do the dishes. What do you guys think?"

"That's a good idea, Coach." Ryan cleared his plate from the table.

"I thought of it first." Andrew nearly tripped over his own feet, trying to get to the dishwasher before Ryan.

Thankful that Andrew didn't fall down and crack open the other side of his head, Melanie smiled as she went into the adjoining den and settled on the couch. So much for the true spirit of cooperation. Nothing much had changed. Her boys were still trying to outdo each other, but at least, it was in a noble effort.

While Nathan and the boys worked in the kitchen, Melanie tried not to stew about her upcoming date with Nathan. Her gaze fell on her Bible sitting on the end table. God's word.

Hadn't it taught her to rely on Him and not worry about tomorrow? God had helped her through the death of her husband, so He was surely there now to help her through a new chapter in her life.

"We're done." Ryan bounded into the den.

Andrew flew in right behind Ryan and slid to a stop as he sat on the floor on the opposite side of the coffee table from Melanie. "Now we can play a game."

Melanie looked over her shoulder to check on Nathan. He stood there watching them while that lopsided grin curved his mouth. Then he looked at her, and her heart raced like the boys chasing each other through the house. She swallowed the lump that had formed in her throat. "Do you have time for a game?"

"I do." Nathan sat in the nearby armchair and scooted it closer to the coffee table.

"I'll get the game." Ryan headed toward the basement stairs.

"Me, too." Andrew jumped up and chased after Ryan.

Shaking her head, Melanie decided there was no point in trying to stop him. She ventured a glance at Nathan.

His grin grew wider. "I can see myself in Andrew. I spent my whole life trying to keep up with my big brother, too."

"I hope they don't argue over who gets to carry the game."

"I'm sure they'll work it out."

"Did you and your brother work it out?"

Nathan laughed. "Yeah, after we grew up."

Putting her head in her hands, Melanie groaned. "You mean it's not going to get better?"

"It'll get better. It just might take a while." Nathan chuckled. "You'll survive. My mom did."

Melanie looked up and tried to give Nathan an annoyed look. "You are absolutely *no* help."

"Sure I am. I cleaned up after supper."

"And I thank you for that."

Ryan came charging back into the room, the game box under one arm. He slapped it on the coffee table. "Here it is."

Without the slightest hint of a complaint, Andrew quickly knelt down and started setting up the game. She couldn't believe it. Her boys were actually cooperating for a change. Grinning, Nathan winked at her.

When the game was set up, Nathan eyed the boys. "Since your mom was the winner last time, she gets to pick her color first."

Melanie almost sighed out loud, but caught herself just in time. This man was too thoughtful. "I'll take red."

"Blue." Andrew grabbed for the blue pieces.

"Green." Ryan looked at Nathan. "Guess Coach has to take yellow."

"I like yellow."

The game proceeded with much laughter and teasing as Ryan and Andrew tried to outdo each other. Melanie figured as long as they were laughing the competition was good. And Nathan's companionship made everything better.

"Are you boys going to ride in the kids' parade during the Fourth of July festivities in town?" Nathan drew a card and moved one of his pieces to the appropriate space on the board.

"I'm not familiar with that parade. What does it involve?" Melanie took her turn.

"Haven't you been to the Kellerville Fourth of July activities?" Nathan asked.

"Not the parade. Two years ago we went to the fireworks." Melanie had done that for the boys even though she hadn't really felt like celebrating anything only months after Tim's death. "Then last year we were with Tim's parents in Columbus for the Fourth of July."

"Are you going to be here this year?" Nathan drew a card and groaned when he had to move one of his pieces back four spaces.

"Yes."

"Then you'll have to have Ryan and Andrew decorate their bikes for the parade."

"But don't they have a parade with floats and marching bands and stuff?" Melanie knit her eyebrows.

"Yeah. That's the big parade they have in the morning, but in the afternoon, they have a kids' parade—kids on bicycles, tricycles, Big Wheels, wagons or whatever they bring to ride all decorated in red, white and blue. They make one trip around the square. Parents usually go with the younger kids. They've had it ever since I was a youngster."

Andrew scrunched up his face. "That's a *looong* time ago."

Nathan chuckled and playfully punched Andrew on the arm. "Are you trying to make me feel old?"

Innocence painted all over his face, Andrew looked up at Nathan. "You're a lot older than me."

Nathan let out a guffaw. "You've got me there. I am a lot older than you."

"But he's not as old as Grandpa Drake," Ryan said.

"Thanks, I think." Nathan tousled Ryan's hair.

"I want to decorate my bike and do the parade." Andrew made his move and sent one of Ryan's game pieces back to the home space. "I'm winning."

Ryan made a face at Andrew. "The game's not over."

"Okay, boys, if you're going to argue the game *will* be over."

"We won't argue." Andrew looked contrite. "Can we do the parade, Mom?"

"If you boys show me your best behavior, you can be in the parade."

"Would you like to go to the parade with me?" Nathan glanced from the boys over to Melanie. "I could pick you up in my SUV and put the bikes in the back. We can go to my house, which is close to town. Then you boys can ride your bikes…in fact, we can all ride bikes to town." Nathan looked at Melanie. "I have a bike for you, too."

Melanie nodded. "Okay, but only if they stay out of trouble until then."

"We will." Ryan gave Andrew a high five.

During the rest of the game, Melanie smiled to herself every time the boys started to get upset, then stopped, because they remembered that their participation in the parade was on the line.

When the game finally ended, Melanie raised her hands in victory. "I'm champ again. Guess you guys can't beat me."

"Do we have time to challenge you to another game?" Grinning, Nathan raised his eyebrows.

"We do." Melanie started setting up the board for a new game.

A jovial battle ensued as they moved their pieces around the board. In the end, Melanie won again.

Nathan narrowed his gaze as he looked at Melanie. "How do you do that?"

"You mean win every time?" Melanie shrugged. "I think it's because you guys are so busy knocking each other off that you forget about me."

"Oh, so I've been too nice to you in this game."

Melanie chuckled. "Maybe."

"Next time you'd better beware."

"I'll be ready." Melanie put the last piece in the box and replaced the lid. Although she'd been trying not to think about their upcoming date, she still wondered when Nathan was going to talk to the boys. She didn't want to seem pushy by bringing it up. "Okay, Ryan and Andrew, it's time to say good night to Coach and get ready for bed."

"Do we…" Ryan's sentence trailed off along with the whine in his voice. He glanced at Melanie as if to see whether he was in trouble, then turned to Nathan. "Good night, Coach."

Andrew popped up from the place where he'd been sitting. "Thanks for playing games with us again."

"Before you guys head to bed, I've got something important to ask you." Standing, Nathan gestured toward Melanie. "That is, if your mom will give me a few more minutes to talk to you."

Melanie nodded, relief sweeping through her mind. Finally, he was going to say something about their date.

Nathan sat again and motioned for the boys to come closer to his chair. "Remember when you asked me whether I liked your mom?"

"Yeah, and you said you did." Andrew nodded, giving Nathan a knowing look.

"Since I think your mom is a very nice lady, I'd like to take her out to eat and to a movie. Just the two of us. Is that okay with you guys?"

Melanie's heart sat in her throat as she watched Nathan and her boys. Nathan actually looked a little nervous. His anxiety about her boys' approval touched her deep inside. He was definitely a man she could truly fall in love with.

Andrew's expression didn't change. "You mean like a date?"

"That's right."

"I think that's a good idea, if you take her some place extra nice—not the Dairy Barn."

Melanie could tell that Nathan was holding back a smile, as he tried to keep his expression serious. "Is it okay if I take her to an extra-special restaurant and a movie?"

Ryan nodded. "That's good. That's what our dad would've done."

Wishing Ryan hadn't mentioned Tim, Melanie waited for Nathan's reaction. He probably didn't wanted to hear about Tim, either, but talking about him was as natural as breathing for her sons.

Nathan reached over and ruffled Ryan hair. "Your dad was a smart man. He obviously knew how to treat your mother right. What would you think if I took your mom on a date to New York City in my plane?"

Ryan's eyes grew wide. "You can fly a plane?"

"I can. Would you like to go up in it?"

"Awesome!" Andrew looked at Melanie. "Mom, could we do that sometime?"

Melanie shrugged, realizing she had a lot to learn about Nathan. "We'll see. Good behavior goes a long way toward that goal."

"I'm going to be really good." Scrunching up his face, Andrew turned his attention back to Nathan. "Are you guys going to get all mushy and kiss and stuff?"

Heat rising in her cheeks, Melanie figured her face must be about the color of one of the red game pieces she'd played with earlier.

Nathan didn't blink an eye. "Would it be all right if I kiss your mom?"

Andrew appeared to be thinking really hard. "I suppose… it might be okay if you don't get too mushy."

Nathan took several seconds to answer, again obviously holding back his amusement. "And what do you think is too mushy? Because I don't want to get it wrong."

"You gotta not kiss too long." Andrew wagged a finger at Nathan.

Nathan nodded. "Okay, so I have to keep the kiss short."

"Yeah." Ryan jumped into the discussion. "And no picking her up and carrying her around."

Melanie wished the den floor would open up and drop her into the basement. Ryan was obviously remembering the night when she and Tim had come home from celebrating their tenth wedding anniversary. A nightmare had awakened Ryan. He'd come into the living room just in time to witness Tim kissing her as he picked her up, intending to carry her to bed. The memory made her blush even more. She had to put an end to this conversation. "Okay, guys, I'm sure Coach understands your rules for dating, and it's past time for you to get to bed."

"'Night, Coach. See you tomorrow at church." Andrew went up and shook Nathan's hand, as if they'd just made some kind of pact. Ryan did the same, and the two boys marched off toward their bedrooms.

When Melanie finally found the nerve to look Nathan in the eyes, he was smiling as he lounged against the breakfast bar that separated the kitchen from the den. She tried to smile back. "Sorry about that."

"I'm not." Nathan stepped closer. "It showed me how much your boys love you."

A lump rising in her throat, Melanie blinked rapidly as she tried to hold back the mist in her eyes. "I know they do, but I hope it doesn't make you uncomfortable for them to keep talking about Tim. I guess that includes even me."

Nathan reached out and took her hands in his. "That's okay. Right now we're just trying to figure out where our current feelings might lead us. So don't ever worry about you or your boys mentioning Tim. He was a part of your life that you won't ever forget. I understand that."

Swallowing hard, Melanie gazed up at Nathan. He made her feel alive again after two years of just going through the motions of living. "Thanks for being so understanding. That means a lot to me, and I'm looking forward to next Saturday. What time should I be ready?"

"I made reservations at the restaurant in Lebanon for six-thirty. It takes about forty-five minutes to get there, so I'll pick you up at five-thirty." He dropped her hands. "But one of these days I will take you to New York City when I go to visit Marcus."

"That would be nice, I think. I've never done much flying."

"Then I'll definitely have to take you up sometime."

For a second, Melanie thought he might kiss her—one of those short kisses that would meet Andrew's approval, but, instead, he took a step toward the front hall. Feeling foolish, she turned swiftly so there could be no possible chance that he might see thoughts of kisses registering in her eyes. She scurried to the front door and switched on the porch light. "That sounds good. I'll call the sitter and let her know what time."

"Good night." He jogged to his car and waved as he got in.

Melanie stood on the porch and watched him drive away with a gamut of emotions washing over her. She couldn't deny the anxiety involved with starting a new relationship. Part of her relished the thought, but the other part worried about what Tim's parents would say. How would they react to her having a new man in her life?

Vowing not to fret anymore about what the Drakes' reaction might be, Melanie went to tuck her boys into bed. She would enjoy her date with Nathan without allowing expectations to interfere. After saying his prayers and kissing her good night, Ryan didn't say much about her going on a date. She wondered what thoughts were running through the little boy's head.

When she went into Andrew's room, he was lying there staring at the ceiling. He looked so somber, as if he were contemplating some deep philosophical question. Sometimes he was such a serious little fellow. She waited a few seconds, but he didn't say anything. "Ready to say your prayers?"

Nodding, he knelt beside his bed, and she joined him. Tonight as she listened to the prayers of her children, she realized that, not only had she been going through the motions of her everyday life, but she'd also been going through the motions of her spiritual life, even though she attended church, read her Bible and prayed. She'd started the grief recovery group, but she hadn't been honest with herself about her grief, her fears or her future. Her budding relationship with Nathan had opened her eyes.

After Andrew finished his prayers, he scrambled into bed. Tucking the covers up under his chin, she leaned over and gave him a good night kiss. "Sweet dreams."

"Mommy, are you going to marry Coach Nathan, so he could be our dad?" Wide-eyed, Andrew gazed at her.

If Melanie hadn't been holding on to the headboard, the impact of Andrew's question could have knocked her off her feet. Trying to figure out how to answer her son's inquiry, Melanie sat on the bed next to him. She pushed his hair back off his forehead, revealing the stitches from his fall. She gave him another kiss. "Sweetheart, it's not that simple."

Andrew frowned. "But he's taking you on date, and he wants to kiss you."

Melanie was at a loss as to how to explain adult relationships to a seven-year-old boy. She was having enough trouble figuring out how to deal with the newness of this whole dating thing herself. She let out a heavy sigh. "Andrew, people go on dates to get to know each other better."

"But you know Coach Nathan already."

"Yes, that's true, but—" Melanie sighed again, feeling more

helpless than ever. "But we don't know whether we want to get married. Going on dates will help us figure that out. That's what your dad and I did before we got married."

"How soon will you know?"

Pressing her lips together to keep from laughing in frustration, Melanie shook her head. Why couldn't his questions be easy? "I can't tell you that. We'll have to wait and see."

"God knows. So I'm going to pray that He lets you know soon."

"Yes, He does. So we'll all have to pray about it." She gave Andrew another kiss and a hug. "Good night."

As Melanie left Andrew's bedroom, her son's simple wisdom soaked into her brain and melted her heart. God knew what she needed and whether Nathan was part of that, so why couldn't she leave all of it in God's hands? Maybe Andrew's prayers would help her find the answers to the questions that plagued her.

Despite Nathan's kindness and her little boy's heartfelt wish, she still worried about letting herself fall for another man whose family would probably disapprove of her upbringing, her background and everything else about her. The problem was not only trying to figure out her relationship with Nathan but also trying to figure out how it affected the people around them—her boys, Nathan's parents and the boys' grandparents.

Her background didn't seem to bother Nathan, at least what he knew of it, just as it hadn't bothered Tim. But Tim's parents were a whole different matter. John and Ginny Keller also seemed to like her, but would their opinion change when they found out she was the daughter of a drug-addicted woman who had died of an overdose? Melanie hurt when she thought about it.

When she'd met Tim, she'd fallen fast for him. She'd known

from the first date that they were meant for each other. Was it happening all over again with Nathan? Was it possible to have two great loves in a lifetime?

Chapter Twelve

The afternoon sunshine peaked through the blinds into Melanie's bedroom and fell on the bed where she'd laid the multicolored chiffon dress. Tonight she was going on a date with Nathan. Hardly able to contain her excitement, she felt like a teenager again, getting ready for her first date.

Even though she'd seen Nathan at church this past Sunday and at the boys' ball games during the week, she'd barely had a chance to talk with him because he'd had to rush off for meetings. She knew he was very busy with all that was going on at the bank, but she missed having him there when they went to the Dairy Barn for ice cream.

She thought about Nathan's plans to go to a wonderful historic restaurant in a nearby town, then drive back to Kellerville for a late-night movie at the local theater. Melanie could hardly wait. Silly as it was, she felt like a princess in a fairy tale getting ready for the ball. She was going to wear a beautiful new dress and high heels. No scrubs. No practical shoes. Wrapping her arms around her shoulders, she twirled around like a kid.

"Mom, what are you doing?"

Melanie heard Ryan's voice and stopped midspin and looked

toward the doorway as he rushed into the room. "Laying out my dress for tonight."

"How come you're getting it out now?"

"I didn't want to leave everything to the last minute like you boys insist on doing so often." Melanie knew there was no way her son was going to understand the exhilaration that pulsed through her veins when she thought about tonight.

Ryan shrugged. "Is it okay if Andrew and me go down to Jordan's house to play?"

"Are you done with your chores?"

"Yeah. My room's clean, and I cleaned my part of the bathroom. Andrew's doing his part now."

"Good, but I'll call Jordan's mother first to make sure it's okay with her." Melanie looked up the phone number in her little book. As she punched in the number, Andrew joined them. The boys hovered close while Melanie talked on the phone. When she was finished, she looked their way. "Okay, you may go."

"Yay!" the boys shouted as they started to run from the room.

Melanie nabbed Ryan by the back of his shirt. Both boys stopped and looked at her as she pointed at the clock on the nightstand. "It's almost three o'clock. I want you home at five, not a minute later. I'm ordering pizza for you guys for supper. Don't be late."

The boys let out another cheer as they raced away. Melanie sat on the bed, then flopped back with her hands above her head. Closing her eyes, she let images of Nathan roll through her mind as she remembered all of the thoughtful things he'd done since that day at the bank. He was the kind of man she needed—the kind of man the boys needed. Was this God's plan?

Sitting up, she glanced at the clock. Enough daydreaming. She finished getting the rest of her clothes together, then prepared to take a shower and do her hair. As she turned on the shower, the phone rang.

She hurried into the bedroom to answer it. "Hello."

"Hi, Melanie. This is Nathan."

Her heart hammered at the sound of his voice that resonated with an odd tone for some reason. "Hi."

There was silence.

Why wasn't he talking? Dread filled Melanie's mind. "Is everything all right?"

"I'm sorry to call so late…" The line grew quiet again. "I—I'm going to have to cancel our date. I'm not feeling well."

Melanie sat on the bed to get off her shaky legs. "I'm sorry. What's wrong? Can I get you something—do something to help you?"

"No. There's nothing you can do. I hate this. Maybe we can reschedule."

"Sure. I understand." But she didn't understand why he'd said maybe—maybe they could reschedule. Why not let's reschedule? "I hope you feel better soon."

"Thanks. I'll talk to you later."

"Okay."

"Bye."

The phone went dead, and Melanie's hopes went dead, too.

Like an automaton, she put the phone in its cradle. Staring at the dress lying next to her on the bed, she ran her hand over the silky material. She felt like a fool. She'd spent way too much money on this dress—one that Juliane had special ordered for her.

What would Juliane say now? What would the boys say? Why was she thinking this way? Nathan had a legitimate excuse for calling off their date. He was sick. But why did she think something else was going on with him? Had he changed his mind about wanting to go out with her?

She finally realized the shower was still running. As she turned it off, the misery that had been building up inside her overwhelmed her. She burst into tears. Covering her face with her hands, she sank onto the bathroom rug and sobbed her heart out. As she cried she wasn't even sure this was only about Nathan. Maybe it was about the people who'd abandoned her during her life, all the disappointments and all the heartaches she'd endured. She just didn't know.

As she sat there, she raised her head and wiped her eyes with the back of her hand. She shouldn't be crying. There were a lot of people who were worse off than she was. Nathan, for one. He was sick.

She'd put so much expectation into this evening. Now her hopes were dashed, and those old doubts and fears were working overtime in her mind, making her feel sorry for herself. But she was a grown-up, not some schoolgirl whose date didn't show up.

Glancing out the bathroom door, she caught sight of the clock. When the boys returned home, she didn't want them to see her crying. She didn't want to have to explain anything about Nathan when she wasn't sure she knew the whole story. Was she going to sit here and let her worries and doubts win, or was she going to get ready anyway and find out where she stood with Nathan?

Releasing a harsh breath, she got up, grabbed a tissue and wiped her nose and eyes. She was going to pull herself together and make the most of this evening. After all, she still had a sitter. She stared at herself in the mirror. Her eyes were red and puffy. If the boys walked in right now, they'd know for sure that she'd been crying. She didn't want that to happen. Maybe a quick shower was in order anyway.

A half hour later as Melanie put the finishing touches on

her makeup, she heard the slamming of the door and the noisy clomping of feet. Her children were home. She ran a brush through her hair one more time, then went out to greet them. They were coming down the hall as she stepped out of her bedroom.

"Hi, Mom. We're home right on time."

"That's good. Go wash your hands. The pizza will be here about the time the sitter arrives, which will be at any moment." Melanie started for the kitchen.

Ryan caught up to her and tugged on one arm. "Mom, how come you're not wearing your pretty dress?"

Melanie smiled at the fact that Ryan noticed. At least there was something to cheer her up, even though it would require an explanation that she really didn't want to make. "Nathan isn't coming to pick me up tonight because he's sick, so I'm going over to his place to cheer him up."

"Can we go?" Andrew asked. "I want to cheer him up, too."

"No, he's not feeling well, so he probably doesn't want a lot of company."

"Then why are you going?" Andrew knit his eyebrows.

Melanie searched for an answer. Why did Andrew always seem to ask tough questions? "Because sometimes when you're sick you need some special attention."

"I can do that."

"I know you can, but people who aren't feeling well don't usually want a lot of noise." Melanie hunkered down next to Andrew. "I know you care about Coach Nathan, and you want to help, but you'd be bored going over there. He's not going to be up to playing games with you. Do you understand?"

Andrew nodded. "I know what I can do. I can pray for him."

"That's a very good idea. I'll tell Nathan you're praying for him. I'm sure that'll make him feel better."

Moments later, the sitter and the pizza arrived. Melanie made sure the sitter had instructions for the boys and wrote her cell number on the pad by the kitchen phone.

Melanie kissed the boys goodbye. "Be good. I love you."

"I love you, too." Andrew gave her a hug.

Ryan did the same, and then both boys dug into the pizza.

"Bye, Mrs. Drake. I'll make sure the boys are in bed on time."

"Thanks, Sarah. I'll be home by midnight."

As Melanie backed her car into the street, she wasn't sure what she was going to do. She wanted to see Nathan, but as she rethought her initial reaction to the situation, she didn't know whether he would welcome her company, either. He was not feeling well.

Driving through town, she let her mind wrap around her options, none of which seemed ideal. She could show up at Nathan's place unannounced. If she did that, he might think she was overstepping. She could call, but he might refuse to see her, insisting that she shouldn't go out of her way. Or she could grab something to eat and join the folks strolling around the square as they enjoyed a warm summer evening. Then she could go to that late-night movie. If she did that, what would she tell the boys when they asked about Nathan?

Why had she gone off without thinking this thing through first? She'd let her unruly emotions rule her brain. Not a good thing.

Finally, she parked her car near the café where the Kellers had celebrated Addie's birthday. Melanie's stomach chose that moment to growl, as if it knew where she'd stopped. She decided to get something to eat and really take the time to properly weigh her options and make a decision.

As she sat on one of the benches in the square, she took in the decorations for the upcoming Fourth of July festivities already evident on the buildings and street corners. The viewing stand for town dignitaries had been erected near the gazebo that sported red, white and blue banners. How was Nathan's illness going to affect his invitation to pick up Ryan and Andrew's bikes for the kids' parade?

Biting into her sandwich, Melanie replayed her phone conversation with Nathan. She'd let the disappointment short-circuit her thinking. She should've insisted on seeing him and not let her doubts about their growing relationship color everything. The fog of her uncertainty had led to a lot of unclear thinking, but not anymore.

She grabbed her cell phone from her purse. Taking a deep breath, she punched in Nathan's number. She liked Nathan, maybe even loved him. So she wasn't going to let her doubts win.

Rubbing a hand across his stubble-covered chin, Nathan sagged back against the couch. The abdominal pains had subsided, but he was prepared for more at any moment. Why did he have to have a flare-up of his Crohn's disease now, just before his date with Melanie?

Four days ago when he'd awakened with the uncomfortable cramping in his abdomen, he prayed that this flare-up wouldn't spell the end of his relationship with Melanie. Even though the doctor had immediately called in a prescription and Nathan had started on the prednisone that day, the symptoms had not subsided as quickly as he'd hoped—definitely not enough to go on a date without having to spend every minute worrying about the location of the nearest restroom.

He knew that tension often caused a flare-up of his Crohn's disease. And he'd let the anxiety over the bank audit stress him out completely. The whole thing was a vicious cycle.

For the past several years, he hadn't achieved much balance in his life. He realized his priorities had been out of whack for too many years. Not only had he put the bank before anything else, he'd neglected his relationship with God. Sure, he'd gone to church, but he'd only been putting in his time. Spending time with Melanie had made that more and more clear.

Since his breakup with Andrea, he'd chained himself to the bank. Work made him forget the heartache, at least for a while, and then the long hours had become a habit he had no real reason to break. He wanted to get off the merry-go-round, but he hadn't known how until he'd started finding time to spend with Melanie and her boys. He'd discovered some tranquility in that association. Taking time off to relax with them had helped to give him a better perspective about his life. But how would she react when she found out about his less than perfect health?

While Nathan let the question roll through his mind, the phone rang. As he picked it up, he noticed the caller ID. Melanie. Probably just calling to check on him because she was a caring person. Picking up the phone, he welcomed the chance to undo any hurt that might have resulted from his earlier, rather abrupt phone conversation with her.

"Hello."

"Hi, Nathan. It's Melanie." She gave him no chance to respond. "Could you use some T.L.C.? If you don't have anything contagious, I'd like to come over. I want to see you."

Despite the bravado of her statement, he could hear the uncertainty in her voice. He didn't want her to feel hesitant about seeing him even though he was unsure how to proceed himself. Here was the moment of truth. If he intended to have a relationship with Melanie, she would have to know about his Crohn's disease. It was something he would have to deal with for the rest of his life. Now Melanie would know the truth.

"Nathan? Are you still there?"

"Yeah. I'm here, and I'm not contagious. And I want to see you, too."

"Thank you. I'll be over in a few minutes."

"Do you know where I live?"

"I know your address."

"Good. It's the blue house with the black shutters in the middle of the block."

"Okay, I'm on my way."

After Nathan ended the call, he looked around his living room. It was a mess, but he didn't have the energy to do anything about it. He was a wreck. His house definitely looked like a bachelor lived there. Melanie was going to see him at his worst. After that, if she still wanted to date him, he would know she really cared about him.

He had to admit that he didn't understand why God had allowed him to have Crohn's disease or why that had resulted in his breakup with Andrea. Now he faced the possible end to his hopes about Melanie. He didn't want this stupid disease to ruin everything with her, too. Was that possible? Would Melanie flee as Andrea had? In a few minutes, he was going to get his answer.

Driving through the quiet, older neighborhood a few blocks from the center of town, Melanie looked for the little blue bungalow with the black shutters. When she spotted it, she parked her car in front of the walk that led to the porch. The small yard was neatly manicured. Marigolds formed a colorful row of oranges and yellows in contrast to the greenery of the shrubs that lined the house behind them.

She realized there was a lot about Nathan Keller that she didn't know. Would she get to know him better tonight? That's what she wanted.

Gathering the balloon bouquet, which she'd purchased at the discount dollar store on the town square, she got out pulling the balloons with her. With a tight hold on the strings that bound them together, she took a calming breath and climbed the steps to the front door. She rang the doorbell and hoped she was doing the right thing. But as she stood there waiting for Nathan to answer, she could hardly breathe.

While her nerves hummed, the front door opened ever so slowly. Nathan poked his head out. The dark stubble that covered his face did nothing to disguise his sunken cheeks. She tried not to let her astonishment show. Something was definitely making him very sick. Then she remembered how his mother had been worrying about his health. Could this be related?

"Hi." She held out the balloons that bobbled their get-well messages in the breeze. "For you."

"Thanks. This is a nice surprise." Taking the balloons, he stood in the doorway. "I don't want you to be shocked when you come in here. Remember, I've been sick."

"What should I expect?" She tried to be nonchalant about his pronouncement.

"A disaster area."

Melanie shrugged. "I've seen plenty of those. You remember that I have two boys."

Chuckling, Nathan stepped inside. "Okay. Come on in."

Melanie followed Nathan into the foyer where a framed poster of the Great American Ball Park hung on the wall straight ahead. That didn't surprise her at all. Holding out one hand, he indicated that she should go into the living room to her left. A brown leather couch and loveseat with a few newspapers on them occupied the space. A couple of books sat on one end table, and a few folders were scattered on the coffee table along with a couple of empty glasses. The room wasn't immaculate, but it was hardly the mess she'd expected.

Turning back to look at him, she smiled. "I think you were exaggerating the mess."

"Yeah." Grimacing, he shrugged. "So you wouldn't think I was a complete slob."

"Well, it worked." Melanie took in the way Nathan's gray T-shirt and black shorts appeared to hang on him. Had he lost weight since the last time she'd seen him? Was that the result of his illness?

Removing the newspapers from the couch, Nathan motioned for her to sit down. He placed the weight that held the balloons on the coffee table as Melanie sat down. The balloons bobbed toward the ceiling, straining against the ribbons that connected them to the weight.

He sat beside her. "Thanks for coming, and thanks again for the balloons."

"You know you didn't have to get sick just to get out of going to that chick flick with me."

Laying his head back, Nathan laughed out loud, then grinned at her. "I'm feeling a whole lot better because you're here cracking jokes."

"I'm glad, but seriously, are you doing any better?"

Nathan shrugged. "A little."

Melanie wasn't sure whether she should ask him what was wrong since he hadn't volunteered any information. "Ryan and Andrew wanted to come, too, but I convinced that you didn't need to be overrun with company."

"I wouldn't have minded."

"But I would have." Melanie wanted to be honest about her reasons for being here. "I wanted to spend some time alone with you. That's why we were going on the date, right?"

"You're right." Nathan gave her that lopsided grin that always made her stomach feel as though she'd been riding a roller coaster.

"Anyway, Ryan and Andrew said to tell you that they are praying for you."

"I can use their prayers."

"I'll be praying, too. I hope you're feeling better soon."

Melanie wanted so badly to ask what was wrong, but he might think she was too nosy if she did.

"So I suppose you're wondering what's wrong with me."

"Yeah, that thought did cross my mind." Had he read the curiosity in her expression?

He stared at her for what seemed like forever without saying anything. He appeared to be apprehensive about telling her. Did he have some life-threatening disease? The thought curdled her insides. She wanted to scream against the unfairness of it all, but she shouldn't jump to conclusions.

Finally, he cleared his throat. "Have you ever heard of Crohn's disease?"

Melanie shook her head, unable to speak. Her heart in her throat, she swallowed hard. Her mind filled with all kinds of terrible scenarios.

Nathan took a deep breath and released it slowly. He looked away, then back at her. "Well, I *have* Crohn's disease. I was diagnosed when I was twenty-eight. So I've been living with it for six years."

"What kind of disease is it?"

"It's a disease that affects the gastrointestinal tract. It's a chronic condition, and there is no cure for it."

Fear knotted in Melanie's midsection. "What does that mean for you?"

"It's generally not life-threatening, but I'll have to live with this for the rest of my life." Nathan sighed. "What I'm experiencing now is what's called a flare-up. I can go for months, maybe years without ever having one, while the disease is under control."

"So why are you having one now?" Melanie couldn't keep the concern out of her voice.

"Most likely stress from the bank audit. Anxiety is a trigger for me."

"You mean not everyone who has Crohn's disease is bothered by stress?"

"Not always. Crohn's is a strange disease."

"Why do you say that?"

"Because not everyone with the disease suffers all of the same symptoms. Fatigue can also be a factor." He waved a hand around the room. "That explains my poor housekeeping."

"I've seen worse at my own house."

"Not when I've been around."

"Fortunately for me." Melanie tried to smile. "Even though there's no cure for Crohn's disease, is there a treatment?"

Nathan nodded. "The treatments vary from patient to patient. I take Asacol to control my Crohn's, but even with that I can have an occasional flare-up. Certain foods can cause problems, but not the same foods for everyone."

"Is that why you don't eat salads?"

"Yeah, I can't eat raw fruits and vegetables."

"I'll have to remember that, so I don't try to feed you something you can't eat." Melanie knit her eyebrows together. "What do you do for the flare-up?"

"My doctor prescribes a steroid. I'm taking that now, and after the flare-up is under control, I'll gradually lower the dosage until I'm no longer taking it."

Melanie wondered whether Nathan thought she was asking too many questions, but she wanted to understand what was happening to this man—someone she'd grown to care for so much. "How often do you have one of these—these flare-ups?"

Nathan shrugged. "It's hard to predict. In the last couple of years I've had three, counting this one."

"How come none of your family or friends has ever mentioned this?"

"Probably because they know I don't like to talk about it, and as long as I was doing okay, there really wasn't any point." Looking into her eyes, Nathan reached over and took hold of her hands. "I should've told you about it, but I didn't know how. And since everything was going well, I didn't see any reason to mention it, either."

She read the sorrow in his gaze. "I understand."

"But it wasn't right of me to start a relationship with you without letting you know." Dropping her hands, he glanced away. "Will you forgive me for keeping that information from you?"

"You're telling me now. That's the important thing." Had his reluctance to tell her about his health problems been based on the fact that she'd already dealt with the death of her husband? Did she dare ask?

"I want to be totally candid about everything."

"Okay." Dread seized her heart. What else was he going to tell her?

"I was afraid to tell you partly because of what happened with Tim. I didn't know whether you'd want to be involved with someone who had health issues."

For the second time tonight, Nathan had answered the question in her mind before she could ask it. She felt as though God was guiding their discussion—having them say exactly what needed to be said. "I'll admit that there was nothing easy about dealing with Tim's death."

"I could tell, and I didn't want to add to your problems." Nathan shook his head. "But Juliane's been bugging me for weeks to ask you out."

Melanie chuckled. "You, too?"

"So she's been working on both of us?" A smile brightened his face.

"Looks that way, but I never said anything to her about our date."

"Me, neither. I figured she'd start crowing about her matchmaking skills if I did. She's already taking credit for getting Elise and Seth together."

"That doesn't surprise me."

Nathan took a deep breath. "I also want you to understand that when I first started having problems six years ago, I had no idea what was wrong. The constant sickness and unanswered problems led to the breakup of a serious relationship I was in at the time. That situation made me reluctant to pursue a new relationship with anyone."

"So you were afraid I wouldn't want to deal with your situation, either?"

"I wasn't sure. And I had come to care a lot about you and your boys, so I didn't want to see this come between us."

"Well, I want you to know that your Crohn's disease is not going to change my mind about anything."

"I know that now." Nathan scooted over on the couch and pulled Melanie into his arms. "I should've known before."

Melanie didn't say anything. She just let Nathan hold her tight. Laying her head on his shoulder, she drank in the warmth of his embrace. She hadn't realized how much she needed this until he'd put his arms around her. The doubts and worries of the day seemed to melt away as they were wrapped in one another's embrace.

Finally, he held her at arm's length and smiled. "Thank you for giving me a second chance."

"I didn't know I was doing that."

"But you were when you insisted on seeing me. I kind of botched calling off the date. I can't imagine what you thought."

Melanie just smiled. There was no way she was going to tell him that she'd cried, but there were some things she did need to tell him. She realized that tonight was about sharing. She was learning a lot about Nathan, but he also needed to know all the good and bad stuff about her life. He knew a little, but not all. But where did she start?

Releasing a shaky breath, she knew she could tell him one thing. "I called because I knew I needed to see you."

"And I'm glad you did."

"Now it's my turn."

A frown wrinkled Nathan's brow. "Turn for what?"

"To tell you about my past."

He shook his head. "What don't I know?"

"You knew I grew up in foster care, but you don't know why, do you?"

"No, should I?"

Not sure exactly how to proceed, Melanie bit her bottom lip. She had to lay it all out there just as Nathan had done when he talked about his Crohn's disease. "You know that Tim's parents don't exactly approve of me."

"And I don't understand that."

"Maybe after I finish telling you about my life, you will." Melanie sighed heavily. "I never knew my father, who probably doesn't even know I exist, or my grandparents. And my mother was addicted to drugs. So I was put in foster care before I started school. I think Tim's parents were afraid that I'd turn out like my mother."

Nathan didn't say anything for a few moments, but his frown deepened. Finally, he shook his head. "I'm sorry, but that's ridiculous."

"They were worried that Tim didn't know me well, enough to be sure, even though we started dating almost a year before we got married."

"Sounds like they were looking for an excuse not to like you. I'm afraid if I ever met them, I might give them a piece of my mind." Nathan shook his head again. "So what happened to your mother? Do you ever see her?"

"She died of a drug overdose when I was eleven." Again

Nathan was silent, and Melanie focused on the painting of a landscape hanging above the fireplace. Although she should be used to people's reactions by now, she hated their pity. Her heart thumped, and she held her breath as she waited for his response.

"Melanie." Nathan said her name almost as if it were a command, but no pity sounded in his voice.

She looked at him. No pity shone in his eyes, either. "Yes?"

"I'm so sorry about your mother."

"Me, too." Slowly, Melanie shook her head. "I remember her holding me and singing to me. She loved me, but she couldn't rid her life of the drugs."

"So did you find a good life in foster care?"

"No."

"Do you mind telling me about it?"

Melanie took in his question with trepidation. She guessed she could manage the short version.

Taking a shaky breath, she met his gaze. "In the beginning I lived in several homes that had lots of foster kids. It was like being in a holding pattern. Nobody really cared about me. Finally, during high school, I lived with only one family who had two other foster kids. Even though I lived with them for almost four years, I wouldn't let myself get too attached to them. I was always afraid I'd eventually get moved. The system made me feel like a helpless pawn. And you know about my going to live with the Millers after that."

"Wow! You've accomplished a lot, considering the way you grew up." He smiled, admiration evident in his eyes as he gazed at her. "You must be proud of your achievements."

She shook her head. "I can't take credit. I have to give credit for any achievements I've made to God and to Tim. I found God and Tim while I was in college."

Slowly shaking his head, Nathan smiled. "You are amazing."

"There's nothing amazing about me. God's amazing."

"You still feel that way even after Tim died?

"Yes, but the first year after Tim's death, I was kind of frozen—just going through the motions of living. Everyone said I was doing so well, but I was empty inside. God was the only one who could fill that hole. I don't understand why Tim died, but I know God gave me a new life in His Son. So I wasn't going to turn my back on Him because my husband died."

"Do you mind telling me how you met Tim?"

"I don't." Melanie knew this was the good part of her life—the part she always liked to share. As Melanie thought about Nathan's request, she realized that thinking about Tim didn't have her fighting back tears. Instead, thoughts about him made her smile. "I'd like to tell you about him."

"Thanks."

Melanie's heart warmed, knowing that Nathan cared about what had happened in her life before they'd met. "When I lived with the Millers they went to the same church as Tim's parents."

"You met him at church?"

"Not exactly. We met at a singles retreat sponsored by the church the summer after I graduated from high school. Tim was home from college for the summer. I think it was love at first sight. We dated through the rest of the summer. We got engaged the following Christmas and got married in June right after he graduated with his MBA."

"That's when you eloped?"

"Yeah, I think that more than anything made Tim's parents dislike me. I was young. Tim was five years older than me, but I knew he was the right man for me. He was wonderful."

Nathan took her hand. "Thanks for sharing that with me.

I barely knew your husband, but Lukas often spoke of him in glowing terms."

"Tim was a wonderful man, and I loved him so much. But I'm ready to start dating again, and I'm glad it's with you."

"Me, too." Nathan pulled her into his arms and kissed her. The kiss was a taste of the future. She knew that, at this time in her life, Nathan was the right man for her, and for her children. She was beginning to believe she could find amazing love twice in her lifetime.

Chapter Thirteen

The following evening, pinks and oranges painted the sky above the darkened tree line at the edge of Melanie's backyard. She drank in the beauty of the sunset—God's handiwork on display. It reminded her of the way He was working in her life.

As Melanie said a silent prayer of thanks for the talk she and Nathan had had last night, he joined her on the deck. She turned to look at him. "Do you suppose the boys will manage to stay through the night on their first sleepover?"

Nodding, Nathan chuckled. "I'm not so much worried about the boys as I am about the mom, in this case."

Melanie gave him a playful swat. "I'm completely okay with them spending the night at Jordan's house."

"I know you are, but I have to tease you a little." He tapped the end of her nose. "I saw that look of concern when you told me about it."

Melanie sighed. "Okay, I admit I was a little anxious."

"I think they'll do fine."

"I know they will, but I was a little worried about Andrew and his stitches." Melanie shook her head. "He doesn't know how to use caution. I keep wondering what else can happen."

"I don't think you want to know. Remember what I said about the emergency room?"

"Yeah, that's why I'm worried. I'm beginning to believe kids, stitches and broken bones all come in one package." Melanie grimaced.

"The joys of being a parent."

Melanie was starting to hope that someday she could share those joys with Nathan. "I'll be so glad when Andrew gets his stitches out. He keeps complaining that they itch."

Nathan put his arm around her waist and pulled her close. "Since I had to cancel our date, I'm glad you were happy to settle for my attempts at cooking rather than going to some place 'extra nice,' as Andrew would say. But I still intend to take you on a special date to the Golden Lamb."

"And I'm looking forward to it." Melanie looked up at him. "I'm glad you're feeling better."

"Me, too. The prednisone has started to work. Today's the first day I've felt good enough to eat a regular meal, but what really makes me feel good is being with you."

"That makes two of us." Melanie heart thudded as she looked at him. "Thanks for supper."

"You're welcome."

"I think you've been hiding your culinary skills."

Nathan laughed. "Then you'd be wrong. Grilled meat of some kind is the only thing I know how to cook."

"And thanks for cleaning up, too." Melanie stood on her tiptoes and kissed him on the cheek.

"Is that all I get for my efforts?"

"Is this what you were hoping for?" Melanie turned and put her arms around his neck. She pulled him close and kissed him on the mouth. As he deepened the kiss, she let the happiness of her relationship with Nathan fill her heart.

The doorbell rang. Melanie and Nathan abruptly ended

their kiss. Nathan narrowed his gaze. "Do you suppose I was wrong and Ryan and Andrew are already coming home?"

"Or one of them has injured himself." Melanie pushed aside the sliding screen door and headed into the house. She flipped on the front porch light. When she opened the door, her breath caught.

Harlan and Georgia Drake stood on the porch.

"May we come in?" Without waiting for an answer Georgia swept past Melanie.

"Sure." Her stomach churning, Melanie stepped aside as Harlan followed his wife. "I—I'm surprised to see you."

"Melanie, who's here?" Nathan stepped around the corner.

"It's the boys' grandparents, Georgia and Harlan Drake." Her shoulders knotting, Melanie tried to smile. "I don't believe you've met them."

Georgia looked Nathan up and down, then turned her attention back to Melanie. "And who is this?"

Before Melanie could say anything, Nathan stepped forward. "I'm Nathan Keller. I'm a friend of Melanie's, and I'm glad to meet you. Ryan and Andrew have spoken of you often."

Barely acknowledging Nathan, Georgia glanced around. "Where are Ryan and Andrew?"

Taking a deep breath, Melanie focused on keeping her smile in place. "They're at a friend's house."

Georgia glanced at her watch. "Isn't it a little late for them to be out?"

"No. I—it's a sleepover."

"You're letting them spend the night somewhere right after Andrew suffered that terrible gash on his head?" Georgia's voice seemed to raise a pitch with each word.

Melanie wanted to yell at Georgia, but getting upset wasn't going to help. Melanie took a moment to calm herself before she said something she would regret. After all, hadn't she been a little worried herself? "Andrew is doing fine. The stitches are coming out on Tuesday. The boys were so excited about spending the night at their friend's house."

"Well." Georgia lifted her chin as her lips tightened. She looked over at Harlan with a nod. "Tell her why we're here."

Harlan's Adam's apple bobbed as he looked at Melanie. He cleared his throat. "We've been concerned about the things going on here lately, and we'd like to talk about it."

Melanie glanced at Nathan. "You don't need to stay for this family discussion."

"Yes, he does." Georgia stepped forward, eyeing Nathan. "From what we understand, our grandsons have become quite attached to you. So we want you to hear what we have to say, too."

Nathan took Melanie's hand and squeezed it. "I'll be glad to stay."

Not wanting to draw the Drakes' ire, Melanie gestured toward the nearby living room. "Okay, let's sit in here."

Georgia and Harlan sat on the couch. As Melanie sat on the love seat, Nathan, with his back to the Drakes, gave her a what's-up look before he sat beside her. He draped his arm across the back of the love seat in a protective gesture.

Scooting forward, Harlan stared at Melanie. "I might as well get right to the point. Georgia and I feel that since Tim's passing, you've had a difficult time raising Ryan and Andrew by yourself." Harlan hesitated, licking his lips. "We believe there are signs of neglect, and we've contacted a lawyer about gaining custody of our grandchildren."

Melanie couldn't believe what she was hearing. Her heart sinking to her stomach, she was afraid she might get sick all over the living room carpet. Her brain frozen with the hurtful words, she couldn't speak.

"You are quite mistaken. Those boys could have no better

mother than Melanie." Nathan lowered his arm from the back of the love seat to wrap around her shoulders.

His words melted Melanie's frozen mind, and she opened her mouth. "I—"

"And don't you think you're going to step in here and usurp our son's place in our grandchildren's lives." Georgia jumped up from the couch and glared at Nathan.

"Please don't do this." Melanie held out her hands.

Ignoring Melanie's plea, Georgia wagged a finger at Nathan. "Judging from what Ryan and Andrew have said, I believe she's spending too much time with you and neglecting those little boys. Andrew fell and cut his forehead wide open because she was paying more attention to you than to them."

Nathan sat forward. "That's an unfair assessment. You weren't there. Melanie does not neglect those boys for any reason. You can ask anyone in this town."

Melanie's mind buzzed. Would a judge believe Georgia's misinterpretation of that event? Would the Drakes call children's protective services and have the boys taken away while they sought custody? The thought curdled her stomach. After growing up in foster care, she would die if that happened. "You're wrong—very wrong to do this."

Anger floated around the room as if it were alive.

Seething inside, Melanie mustered all her dignity as she stood. Fury kept her from fainting on her wobbly legs. She walked over to the fireplace and stepped up on the hearth. Reaching up, she took down the portrait that she had moved from the den into this room just days ago. Slowly she turned and held it out to Georgia. "I know you've always said how much you liked this. It's yours."

Georgia's mouth hung open. "Why are you doing this?"

"Because if you turn this into a custody battle and I win, I don't know whether I'll be able to find it in my heart to forgive you and let you see your grandchildren again. This will be a reminder of what you've lost." Melanie straightened her shoulders, feeling more confident with each word she spoke. "Now please take this and leave my house."

Nathan stood. "I'll escort you."

As Nathan ushered the angry couple out the front door, Melanie sank to the couch. Still shaking with rage, she put her head in her hands. She couldn't believe she had actually told the Drakes to leave. What must they think of her now?

Moments later, Nathan sat beside her and gathered her in his arms. "I'm so glad you told them to leave. That took courage."

"Well, I'm shaking now." She held out a hand to show him.

He took it and held it tight. "Do you think they would have confronted you like that if the boys had been home?"

Taking in his comfort, Melanie shook her head. "I have no idea what they're capable of. No telling what is going through their minds. I can't believe the awful things they said to you."

"I'm more concerned about how they treated you. You have to know, they don't have a chance in court."

"Unless something else happens to one of the boys. Then they'll be pounding on my door again." Melanie shuddered as she placed a hand over her heart. "With Ryan and Andrew, you never know what might happen, and if either one of them is injured again, the Drakes could claim I'm being negligent."

"Don't borrow trouble. That's what Grandma Addie always says."

"I should take her advice, but I feel as though the Drakes will be watching my every move."

"I'm going to be right there with you. I'll do whatever I can to help." He pulled her close again.

"I don't know what I would have done if you hadn't been

here tonight. Thank you." Melanie laid her head on his shoulder and drank in his comforting words. But even with Nathan by her side, she had no idea how she was going to live through this nightmare.

The Fourth of July was in full swing in Kellerville. Almost every house in town sported a flag or patriotic banner, but Nathan couldn't shake the pall that hung over the celebration after last night's threat from the Drakes. No wonder they had intimidated Melanie all of these years. Even the sunshine glinting off the hood of his SUV didn't brighten his thoughts as he turned onto Melanie's street.

When Nathan parked in her driveway, Ryan and Andrew, dressed in red, white and blue T-shirts and shorts, burst out the front door and ran across the yard. Stopping at the edge of the grass, they both started talking at once as he got out of his vehicle.

Nathan held up his hands. "Hey, guys, one at a time. I can't understand anything when you talk over each other."

"I've got my bike ready for the parade." Ryan pointed toward the garage. "Should I get it out?"

Nathan nodded. "Both of you get your bikes, and I'll put them in the back."

Andrew gave Nathan a big hug. "I'm so glad you're not going to die. I prayed lots for you."

"And I appreciate your prayers." Although Andrew's statement puzzled Nathan, he just smiled. At that moment the garage door opened and Melanie appeared. She looked great in her patriotic shirt and shorts, but he saw the sadness in her eyes that even her smile couldn't cover.

"Hi." Melanie pointed toward the garage. "Are you ready to load these?"

Nathan nodded, surveying the bikes decorated with red, white and blue crepe paper threaded through the spokes and streamers hanging from the handlebars. He looked over at Ryan and Andrew. "Hey, you guys did a terrific job with your bikes."

"Thanks. Mom helped us." Ryan raced over to get his bike.

"Good job, Mom." Nathan put an arm around Melanie's shoulders. He really wanted to pull her into his arms and kiss her, reassure her that things would be okay, but he knew there were no guarantees. She was so brave, trying to keep things upbeat for her children.

Nathan opened the hatch on his SUV. After they got the bikes in the back, Nathan helped Melanie transfer the booster seats from her car to his.

As Melanie went into the house to get her purse, Nathan followed. Placing a hand on her shoulder, he brought her to a stop just inside the door. She turned and looked up at him. Putting his arms around her waist, he pulled her closer. "It's going to be all right."

"I wish I could believe that. It's so hard to keep a happy face for the boys."

"We'll do our best today." He put a hand behind her head. "I hope this will make it better. Happy Fourth of July." Nathan lowered his mouth to hers and drank in her sweet lips. He loved her, and he wanted to be there to help her fight her battles. "Too long, too short?"

"Just right." She smiled her sweet little smile that turned him inside out, especially today with all that she was going through. "Thanks for making me smile."

"I have one question to ask."

"What's that?"

"Why did Andrew say he was glad I didn't die?"

Placing a hand over her heart, Melanie grimaced. "Oh, I forgot to tell you. He was so worried about you when I tried to explain that you have Crohn's disease. Poor little guy was thinking about his dad, and when he heard the word *disease*, he thought it meant that you were going to die."

"Does he understand now?"

"I think so. I spent hours searching sites on the internet. I wanted to understand everything about Crohn's disease before I tried to explain it to Ryan and Andrew, so I read everything I could about the disease, and I shared what I could with the boys."

"All the ugly details." Nathan grimaced.

"Maybe not all. I tried to explain that it was like an extremely bad case of intestinal flu. They've both had that, so I thought the comparison would help them to understand."

"And now you understand why I was rather circumspect when I was talking about the symptoms."

"Yeah, I can't imagine what you went through before the doctors figured out what was wrong."

"And I can't imagine what you went through when Tim died, or what you're going through now."

"Well, I know one thing. We know each other a lot better today than we did a week ago."

Nathan nodded. "And that's a good thing."

"Let's go before the boys think we got lost."

When Nathan and Melanie got into the car, Ryan asked, "What took you guys so long?"

"I think they were getting mushy and didn't want us to see." Andrew chortled.

"They're pretty smart." Smiling wryly, Nathan glanced at Melanie and winked. He hoped the boys' cheer would lighten her outlook.

Melanie joined Andrew's laughter, and the sound of their joy wound around Nathan's heart as he backed out of the driveway. He had no doubt that he wanted this woman and her little boys in his life forever. He couldn't imagine life without them now, but he didn't want to rush Melanie into a relationship she wasn't ready for, especially with the Drakes threatening her.

He couldn't believe how much his thinking had changed since the day she'd come to see him at the bank. Nathan promised himself that he would give her all the time she needed to see that he was the right man for her now. But he couldn't shake the feeling that the Drakes' intimidation might ruin everything.

Nathan drove into the alley behind his house and pulled into his detached garage. As the boys scrambled out of the backseat, Andrew pointed to the two bikes sitting against the wall. "Who's going to ride those?"

"Your mom and me." Nathan went over and put an arm around Melanie's shoulders. "This was my sister's bike. What do think?"

Melanie looked at him. "I didn't know you have a sister."

"Yeah, she's a missionary nurse, working in South America."

"I'm learning new stuff about you every day."

"That goes for both of us." Nathan was learning about the important things in life—things he'd taken for granted like God and family. Melanie's statement also reminded him of his earlier thoughts about not rushing things with their relationship. Even though he hated the waiting, he was finally committed to being there for her and the boys. They still had to take time to get to know each other. After taking so many years to find the right woman to share his life, what were a few more weeks or months? They were probably going to seem like an eternity, though.

After they unloaded the bikes from the SUV and Melanie and Nathan moved them into the alley, Nathan closed the garage. "All right, guys, as soon as we get our helmets on, we'll be ready to roll. We'll travel single file with me in the lead and your mom bringing up the rear."

As they started the five-block trip into town, they met numerous people walking or riding bikes to the festivities. Nathan stopped when they reached the square. "From here we'll walk our bikes across the square."

"Okay." Melanie braked, then hopped off her bike. "Where do we go from here?"

"Let's go to the bike rack in front of the bank. We can park the bikes there and stake out a place to watch the parade." Nathan walked beside Melanie as the boys joined them.

Andrew glanced around, wide-eyed. "There sure are a lot of people here."

"This and Winter Festival are the two big events in town. Almost everyone shows up." Nathan remembered what Melanie had said about not wanting to celebrate after Tim's death. Did being here today remind her of the years she'd been too sad to attend the town events? He hoped their new relationship eased that sorrow, but how could it when her mind was filled with the threat of losing her kids?

Melanie put her bike in the rack, then helped Andrew and Ryan put locks on theirs. "I'm excited about seeing the parade."

"Me, too. Jordan told us last night that he's riding on one of the floats." Ryan craned his neck to look down the street. "I'm going to yell to him. I hope he sees me."

"He'll see you if you sit right here on the curb. Your mom and I are going to sit on these." Nathan unfolded a couple of collapsible chairs that he'd carried across his handlebars.

In no time at all, the sidewalk filled up with other townspeople excited to view the parade. While they waited for the parade to start, the boys chattered about baseball, fireworks and what they were going to eat for lunch. Nathan drank in the happiness around him and thanked God for his improved health and his Uncle Joe, who'd sent Melanie to him for financial advice. And he prayed that somehow God would show the Drakes that they were wrong.

Andrew jumped up. "I see the beginning of the parade."

"Okay." Melanie patted him on the back. "Sit here on the curb, and you'll have a front row-seat."

Nathan grinned at Andrew's excitement, remembering the times when he'd felt the same way as a kid. He should cultivate that same attitude going forward in his everyday life. But he was having a hard time dousing his anger over the way the Drakes treated Melanie. It weighed him down as much as his concerns about the bank had in recent weeks. Even though he'd prayed, he was still not giving his problems over to God. Being with Melanie and her boys had made him rethink so much of what he'd been doing. He needed to enjoy today and not worry about tomorrow.

Melanie smiled at Nathan, and he couldn't think of any place he'd rather be. He just wished he could make them a family sooner rather than later. He wished he could take away all of her troubles.

Patience. He had to remember patience.

Chapter Fourteen

Watching the joy on her sons' faces made Melanie glad she'd decided to attend the parade, despite her worries and sleepless night. Jumping up and down, Ryan and Andrew waved at Jordan, who threw candy from the float sponsored by his dad's lumberyard. They marveled at the guys walking on stilts and waved to Juliane, Lukas, Elise and Seth as they sang on the church float.

For her boys' sake, she would enjoy the day and try not to think about the dreadful message Georgia had left on the cell phone. She had made threats, saying if anything else happened to the boys, she and Harlan would call children's services. The woman had to make sure she got in the last word.

Melanie shook away the horrid thoughts and glanced at Nathan, who seemed as absorbed in the parade as her kids. She tapped him on one arm. "When's the bank float coming?"

"It's near the end of the parade."

"Who's riding on it?"

Shaking his head, he chuckled. "Can you believe it? My folks are dressed up like George and Martha Washington and throwing candy from the float."

"I'm sure they're having a good time."

"Yeah, we're supposed to meet them after the parade, so we can eat lunch together."

"Oh, good." Melanie hoped it would be good. Even though Ginny and John Keller had always been nice to her, she couldn't shake the thought that they would be like Tim's parents, especially after last night. She had another worry—how would her boys behave? She couldn't make a good impression if her children were unruly.

When the parade was over, Nathan folded his chair and looked at Melanie. "Let's find my folks. They said to meet them on this side of the gazebo. I can carry your chair if you want."

"Thanks." Melanie handed it to him as she prepped herself to meet Nathan's parents. She tried to tell herself that she had nothing to worry about, but it didn't help.

"Mom, are we going to leave our bikes here?"

"I think so." Melanie looked at Nathan for confirmation.

Nathan nodded. "We'll get them when it's time to line up for the kids' parade."

The foursome maneuvered their way through the crowd that had gathered on the square. Food booths lined the lawn around the square. The delicious aromas wafting through the area made Melanie's stomach growl.

Nathan nudged her. "I heard that. I think someone's hungry."

Andrew laughed as he skipped along. "And I'm hungry, too."

"I see my folks, Uncle Ray, Aunt Barbara and Olivia." Nathan waved. "You go meet them. The boys and I will get some food. What do you want?"

"Surprise me." Melanie wasn't sure she could eat anyway. Her stomach churned. All the things weighing down on her had made her lose her appetite. Having Nathan's parents like her would give her a boost after last night.

Melanie strolled to the spot where his parents and aunt and uncle had set up lawn chairs. When Melanie joined them, Ginny and Barbara, with a little help from Olivia, spread a couple of blankets on the ground.

Ginny approached Melanie and glanced around. "Where did Nathan disappear to?"

"He and my boys went to get food."

Ginny looked back at Melanie. "I guess he's trying to beat the crowd."

"I don't know whether there's any beating this crowd."

At that moment, Juliane, Lukas, Elise and Seth arrived. Olivia ran to greet Seth, and he swept her up in his arms as she giggled. Melanie hugged Juliane and Elise, and joyous greetings spread throughout the group. The four men snagged a picnic table and pulled it near the blankets. Then the men took orders and sauntered off toward the food booths.

As Melanie watched them go, Ginny looked Melanie's way. "Did your boys enjoy the parade?"

Taking in Ginny's interest, Melanie let go of her anxiety. "They did. They're looking forward to the kids' parade."

"Me, too." Ginny clapped her hands. "The kids are so adorable. Seems like yesterday that my kids were decorating their bikes and riding around the square. Nathan used to try to outdo his brother every year."

Chuckling, Melanie nodded. "He told me that."

"You and Nathan have grown close. I'm glad."

"Me, too." Despite Ginny's friendliness, Melanie couldn't stop the worry that slipped into her mind. Would this woman feel the same way when she learned about Melanie's past?

Ginny laid a hand on Melanie's arm. "Nathan has seemed so much happier since you came into his life."

"Thank you. My boys adore Nathan. He's been so good to them."

"I'm glad he's been a help to you." Ginny smiled. "I've

been meaning to talk to you for the longest time. You have a remarkable testimony—how you overcame your troubled childhood and found a new life in Jesus."

Melanie's mind buzzed as she tried not to let her bafflement show. How did Ginny know about her past? Had Nathan talked to his mother since Saturday? Melanie swallowed the lump in her throat. "How do you know about my childhood?"

"About a year ago, I heard you speak to a group of girls from the children's home that the church sponsors."

Melanie remembered speaking at the home in a nearby town, but she didn't remember seeing Ginny Keller. "You were there?"

"I was, and I was so impressed. What a blessing for those girls to hear you!"

"Thank you." After dealing with the Drakes' disfavor, Melanie could hardly believe what she was hearing. "Dr. Joe is a big supporter of that mission and asked me to speak to the group."

"Well, I'm going to have to give my brother a pat on the back."

"He's a wonderful boss." Melanie began to put all the pieces together. Ginny was Dr. Joe's sister. Melanie hadn't made the connection before. She knew that Dr. Joe's family gave a lot of donations to this children's home. Now she understood why Ginny would've been there.

Leaning closer, Ginny cupped one hand near her mouth. "I know, but I can't give him too much praise. It might go to his head."

Before Melanie could make another comment, Nathan and her boys returned. Nathan handed her a box and a drink. "Pulled pork sandwich and fries. I hope you like it."

"Thanks. Sounds good." Melanie's appetite had returned with a vengeance.

After lunch, the kids' parade was a roaring success. Nathan

saved the day when he produced a small camera from the pocket of his shorts when Melanie realized she'd forgotten to bring hers. Everything about this day was turning out perfect. The best part was that Nathan's parents liked her even though they knew about her past. After last night, she'd needed to hear something good. *Thank You, Lord, for giving me this to hang on to.*

The afternoon sped by as the group enjoyed the bands that entertained the crowd. Nathan's dad had brought a small chess set and played a couple of games with Nathan. After they were finished, John showed Ryan and Andrew the chess moves. Again, Melanie took in the love and joy in this family gathering. Today she felt as though she belonged. She wasn't an outsider anymore thanks to Nathan and his parents. She was glad she'd made the effort to put aside her worries and be part of this celebration.

As the activities on the square came to a close, Melanie and Nathan gathered their things and prepared for the ride back to Nathan's house. They made plans to meet everyone at the park on the edge of town for the patriotic concert and fireworks.

"Okay, guys, helmets on, and we ride back home in single file the same way we came."

When they were a block from Nathan's house Ryan tried to ride ahead of Andrew, who was behind Nathan.

"Ryan, stay in single file," Melanie called.

"But, Mom, he's going too slow. He's not keeping up with Nathan."

"He's not that far behind."

"Yes, he is." Ryan peddled passed Andrew, hit a pothole and went flying off his bike. He landed with a thud, and his bike clattered to the pavement.

"Ryan!" Melanie braked and jumped off her bike. While Melanie raced over to Ryan, Nathan and Andrew stopped and got off their bikes. They hovered near as she helped Ryan up.

Melanie held back the scolding she wanted to give Ryan. He'd disobeyed her, and now he was suffering the consequences. She guessed that was enough. She surveyed the scrape on one knee, but she didn't see anything else. "Now you know why I said not to pass Andrew."

Looking contrite, Ryan nodded.

Nathan stepped up beside her. "I've got stuff at the house to put on that scrape."

Melanie sighed. "Okay, let's get back on our bikes."

"But, Mom, my arm hurts." Ryan rubbed it.

"I'm sure it does, but you'll have to get on your bike and ride back to Nathan's house."

After they arrived at Nathan's, they parked their bikes in the garage and went into the house. Nathan quickly brought out some disinfectant to clean the scrape, and he put a bandage over it. Melanie could tell that Ryan was on the verge of tears, but he wasn't going to cry no matter how badly it hurt.

After Nathan finished, a very subdued Ryan sat on the couch. He kept rubbing his arm. "When is my arm going to stop hurting?"

"Do you suppose he could have a broken arm?" Melanie glanced at Nathan, her stomach roiling at the thought. How soon would the Drakes be pounding on her door if Ryan had a broken arm?

"The only way to know for sure is to have an X-ray." Nathan shrugged. "Do you want to take him to the emergency room?"

"We'd better." Sighing, Melanie looked at Nathan. "You're going to get tired of accompanying us to the hospital. Andrew doesn't even have his stitches out, and we have to go back."

Minutes later, Nathan parked in the lot outside of the hospital emergency room. Surprisingly, this time the emergency room was very quiet and Ryan was taken right away to get an X-ray, which showed that he did have a broken arm. The emergency room doctor recommended that an orthopedic surgeon set the arm. So they waited for Dr. Daubenmire, who was on call.

After Ryan's arm was set and put into a cast, Melanie returned to the waiting area with Ryan. "We're all set. Six to eight weeks before the cast comes off."

Andrew ran over to inspect the cast. "Cool. A green camouflage arm sling."

"That may look cool, but I don't think Ryan is feeling too cool." Feeling very tired, Melanie nudged Andrew toward the door. "Let's head home."

As Nathan turned the key and the engine roared to life, he glanced over at Melanie. "While you were with the doctor, I called my folks and told them what happened. And don't worry about the bikes. I'll bring them over after work tomorrow."

"I'm sorry you're not getting to hear the concert and see the fireworks."

"I'd rather be with you."

Melanie tried to smile. "Thanks. You're always there when I need you."

"You're fortunate that Dr. Daubenmire was on call tonight. He's the orthopedic surgeon who put Seth back together again after his terrible car accident. Dr. D. is the best."

"That's good to know. He definitely put Ryan at ease." Melanie turned to look at Ryan, then turned back to Nathan. "The doc gave Ryan some pain medicine, so I think when we get home, I'll put him to bed. Andrew even looks sleepy."

"I'm not sleepy, and now I don't get to see fireworks."

Nathan turned into Melanie's driveway. "The park's not that far from here. We can probably see the fireworks from your deck. Should we check it out?"

"Okay." Andrew jumped out of the car and sprinted to the front door. "Hurry."

Unlocking the front door, Melanie glanced at Nathan. "While I put Ryan to bed, you and Andrew can check out the fireworks."

Andrew raced ahead toward the door leading to the deck. Nathan chuckled. "I don't think there's anything sleepy about that kid. He's wired."

"I'll be out as soon as I get Ryan settled."

Nathan nodded. "I'll be waiting."

Melanie had no trouble getting Ryan into bed. The pain medication was making him drowsy. She kissed him good night.

"I'm sorry, Mommy." The sadness in Ryan's voice brought a lump to Melanie's throat.

"I love you." She kissed him again. "And that's okay. We all make mistakes, just make sure you learn from them."

"'Night, Mommy."

Melanie closed the bedroom door and leaned against it. Ryan's broken arm was nothing earth-shattering. Kids all over the country broke arms every day, but those kids didn't have grandparents like Georgia and Harlan Drake. Fear gripped her like an iron fist, while the thought of Georgia's phone message destroyed her hopes.

Melanie walked through the kitchen to the deck and found Nathan and Andrew spraying themselves with bug repellent. Nathan looked up. "Andrew showed me where it was."

"Yeah, I'm sure the mosquitoes are out in full force tonight."

Andrew settled on one of the deck chairs, and Nathan stepped back toward the door where Melanie still stood. He put an arm around her waist just as the first display of fireworks blossomed into the night sky.

Andrew pointed skyward. "I can see them."

"We sure can."

Nathan pulled her close and whispered in her ear. "This is nicer than fighting the crowds.

"You're right." Melanie wanted to snuggle closer, but she couldn't. Everything she had hoped for Nathan and her was exploding into thin air like the fireworks because of Ryan's broken arm.

Melanie had experienced a wonderful love with Tim, but it had always been marred by the troubled relationship she continued to have with his parents. Now Nathan had come into her life, and his parents didn't care about her background. They liked her for who she was, not where she'd come from or how she'd grown up. But she was going to have to let it all go in hopes that she could keep her kids. How was she going to tell Nathan?

Chapter Fifteen

After Melanie put Andrew to bed, she went back to the deck where Nathan was talking on his cell phone. He looked her way as she drew near and smiled. The night air made Melanie shiver, but not as much as the thought of losing her children. She had worked so hard to be a good mother. How could Tim's parents not see that? How could they be so cruel?

Nathan reached out his hand and pulled her closer as he ended the call. "That was my mom. She called to find out how Ryan's doing."

"Your mom's so thoughtful." Melanie's heart ached as she held Nathan's hand. He cared. His parents cared, and now she was going to have to make a choice. Her kids or Nathan and his big loving family. What kind of choice was that? No choice at all.

Where was God right now? He seemed very far away. She hadn't felt this hopeless when Tim died. God had been there to comfort her then, but she felt no comfort in this situation. She couldn't seem to pray. She didn't know how. God probably wouldn't hear her prayers anyway because she was struggling to find forgiveness for the Drakes. Anger and hurt were the only things in her heart.

Nathan gathered her into his arms. She knew she shouldn't

be taking his comfort when she intended to end the relationship that had barely begun. But she wanted to feel his arms around her one more time.

"Would you like me to help you get a lawyer?" he asked as he continued to hold her.

"No, not now." Knowing she couldn't ask him to help her, she stepped out of his embrace and told him about the phone message Georgia had left. "I can't get my head around why they're making these threats. I still can't believe they're considering this."

"Maybe they won't."

"I'm afraid they will especially since Ryan has broken his arm." She knew she had to end their relationship, but she didn't know how to tell him.

Nathan patted her back, then stepped away. "You've had a stressful day. I'm going to go, so you can try to get some rest."

Melanie touched his arm. "Please don't go yet. There's something I need to tell you."

"What?" Nathan leaned against the deck railing.

Melanie looked at the decking, unable to meet Nathan's gaze. "I think we should cool our relationship…" Pressing her lips together, she closed her eyes. She would not cry.

He stepped closer. "Melanie, why? Is it because of the Drakes?"

She nodded. "Once they find out about Ryan's arm, I'm sure they'll see this as their opening to cast me as a negligent mother. If I want to keep this from going to court, I'll need to make certain…concessions."

Nathan gently lifted her chin with a finger. "I could talk to them."

"No. No. I'm afraid that would only make it worse." Stepping away, Melanie couldn't stand to look at the hurt in his eyes. She covered her face with her hands.

Nathan sighed heavily. "So you want to back away until they cool off or is this forever?"

Not forever. The words hung in Melanie's mind. Lowering her hands, she looked back at him. She bit her lower lip to keep from saying the phrase, because she couldn't make that promise.

When she didn't say anything, Nathan hung his head. "So I guess if I'm out of the picture, the Drakes might be more reasonable. Is that what you're saying?"

His restatement of her words ripped her apart. "Yes. That's the way it has to be."

"I don't want to do this. We can fight them. They can't win. There is no way any court would rule that you're a bad mother." He met her gaze, sorrow radiating from his eyes.

"You're right. They probably can't win, but what will it do to the boys to go through an ugly custody fight?"

"I can't pretend to like this, but I'll do what you want because I care about you and your boys, and I don't want to do anything that would cause you hurt."

Misery filling her entire body, Melanie took a shaky breath and looked out at the darkened yard—the yard where Nathan had first helped Ryan and Andrew play baseball. "Then it's settled. We won't be seeing each anymore?"

"I just want you to remember one thing. If you need me, I'll come running. I'll do anything to help you, and if it means stepping away, that's what I'll do.

Melanie walked to the other side of the deck. "This is the first time since I've been a Christian that I can't seem to pray."

"I'll be praying for you." He came to stand beside her. "What do you want me to tell people? You know they'll ask what happened. What will Ryan and Andrew say?"

Nathan's questions sent a crushing sensation through her chest as if a great weight were pressing down on her. What could he say to his family—all the people she'd come to love? "Tell them the truth. It just didn't work out."

"Okay. I'll see myself out."

Melanie nodded, wishing this would all go away as she watched him walk out of her life. The Drakes had intimidated her for years, and now they had achieved the worst intimidation of all—the threat of losing her children. She couldn't chance it, despite the heartache of losing Nathan.

Why had she come this close to happiness again just to have it shattered?

Nathan headed to the single-engine airplane that he owned with two of his cousins. Over a month had passed since Melanie and he had ended their short-lived relationship. Even though he saw her and the boys at baseball and church, he missed sharing a meal or an outing with them. His life wasn't the same without them in it.

Although the banking convention in Columbus the past few days had served to take his mind off Melanie for a few hours, she was still often the center of his thoughts when he was alone. He wanted her to have a wonderful, carefree life, and he wanted to be part of it. Now that seemed like an impossible dream.

He tried not to think of the plan he'd had to ask Melanie to marry him on her birthday just weeks away. That plan was history—swallowed up in the vengeance of two hateful people. At least, with Andrew's cut healed, and Ryan's cast off, the Drakes had had no opening to make new threats.

Whenever Nathan thought about Melanie and her boys, he wanted to lash out at the unfairness. They were friendly but reserved when their paths crossed. Their lives were going on without him, so maybe things had worked out for the best, except he was running on empty. He'd been living with this knot in his heart, and he didn't know how to untie it.

Like so many things he did these days, flying made him think about Ryan and Andrew. He'd had dreams of one day helping them learn to fly, just as he'd helped them learn how to water-ski. But those dreams faded. He thought he'd done the right thing when he'd agreed with Melanie to end their relationship, but as the days went by, he wasn't sure. He'd been praying for answers. He'd even been praying that he could forgive the Drakes and make them see how wrong they were. But answers and forgiveness seemed far away.

As he took off and the plane soared into the sky, he tried to let the exhilaration that he always got from being airborne fill his mind. The day was perfect for flying—clear blue skies as far as one could see. But nothing took away his sadness when he thought of Melanie.

About thirty-five minutes into his forty-five minute flight the engine sputtered. Immediately, he checked for icing, but the engine continued to sputter. Nathan prayed. *Lord, help me through this.*

When the engine completely stalled, he called in a May Day to the Kellerville airport. He prayed some more.

The tower responded. "We have you on a visual, and the runway is clear."

At that moment, he realized the plane was losing altitude too quickly and he couldn't make it to the airport. With the forest below, he searched for a clearing where he could land the place. As he surveyed the space, only a small opening came into view, and he knew he had to make a crash landing area in the woods. Stopping the plane before it collided with the denser part of the forest necessitated that he put it between two trees.

Nathan's life blurred before him. If God saw fit to bring him through this, Nathan wasn't going to waste any time. He was going to tell Melanie that he'd been wrong to stop seeing her. He loved her and wanted to marry her. He wanted to stand beside her forever. They could stand up to the Drakes together and win. One last prayer flitted through his mind before the impact ripped off the wings, leaving the fuselage intact. Nathan's head smashed into the instrument panel. He faded from consciousness.

Her heart pounding, Melanie held her boys' hands as she walked into the emergency waiting room. Juliane, who was visiting with Ginny, rushed up to her. "He's doing fine and wants to see you."

"He's been asking for you ever since I got here." Ginny gave Melanie a hug. "His dad's with him now. Follow me."

Ryan tugged on her arm. "Come on, Mom. You heard them. He wants to see us."

Her mind spinning, Melanie followed Ginny. Melanie wasn't sure what she was going to say to Nathan or how she was going to say it, but she had decided to quit being a coward. She was tired of letting the Drakes intimidate her and tell her how to live. She wanted Nathan in her life, and she was going to let him know.

Pushing the curtain aside, Ginny nodded for Melanie and her boys to go in. Nathan smiled when he saw them, and Melanie's heart did a little flip-flop. Dropping her hands, Ryan and Andrew scrambled to beat each other to Nathan's bedside.

As the boys started to pepper Nathan with questions, Ginny touched Melanie's arm and mouthed, "He needs you." Then she and John quietly slipped out of the cubicle.

Blinking back tears, Melanie listened to her little guys interact with Nathan. She had to make him see that they belonged together no matter what Harlan and Georgia Drake said or did. She'd been wrong to back away from him. She'd been miserable without him. And today she could have lost him for good.

Andrew gazed at Nathan with awe. "You crashed your plane?"

Still smiling, Nathan nodded and pointed to his head. "And now we match. Stitches. But I still got you beat." He held up both hands. "Ten."

"Did it bleed all over like mine?"

"I don't know. The crash knocked me out. When I woke up, they already had me in this thing." Chuckling, Nathan pulled on his hospital gown. "They're keeping me here for a few hours just to watch me before they let me go."

"What are they watching?" Concern painted Andrew's voice.

"Just checking me over to make sure I'm okay."

"You look okay to me, except those stitches." Andrew rubbed the scar from his stitches. "I know what that feels like."

"Is your plane ruined?" Ryan asked, vying for Nathan's attention.

"Yeah. One of my cousins who works at the airport tells me that I clipped the wings off when I crashed it. And the front is just hanging there. He says I'm lucky to be alive."

"I think God saved you."

"I believe He did, too. He wanted to make sure I got back here so I could be with you guys." Smiling, Nathan patted Andrew on the head, then looked up at Melanie.

Her insides were a jumble of zinging nerves, pounding heart and racing pulse, but she managed to smile back. Was he saying what she thought he was saying? Swallowing a lump in her throat she stepped closer.

Nathan reached out his hand, and she took it. "Hey, guys, will you let me talk to your mom?"

Melanie glanced from her boys to Nathan. "I'll take them out to the waiting room, okay?"

Andrew poked Ryan on the arm. "I think they're going to get mushy."

"Yeah." Giving his brother a knowing look, Ryan nodded as Melanie escorted the boys out to the waiting area where she left them with Juliane.

When Melanie returned, Nathan was still chuckling. "Now I know why I've missed those kids."

"Never a dull moment."

"And I've had a lot of those lately." Nathan held out his hand again. As Melanie placed her hand in his, he pulled her closer until she was leaning against the bed. "I need a hug."

Melanie furrowed her brow. "Is it safe? Will I hurt you?"

"You'll hurt me if you don't hug me."

She gave him a quick hug and savored the warmth of his touch—the shelter of his arms for those few seconds. *Lord, thank You for keeping him safe.*

She stepped back. "We…"

"We…" They both started talking at once, then laughed.

Nathan held out his hand. "You first."

"Okay. I wanted to talk with you alone because I didn't want to say anything bad about the boys' grandparents in front of them."

"Yeah. That can be a difficult task." Melanie smiled wryly.

Nathan took her hand again. "Even though I've been praying a lot lately, it took this crash for God to finally get my attention. I knew if I survived, I had to tell you I was wrong—"

"No, I'm the one who was wrong." Melanie placed her free hand over her heart. "I should have been stronger. I shouldn't have let the Drakes intimidate me that way. I shouldn't have asked you…asked you to back away."

"I understand." Nathan pulled her close. "You've been the

strong one, having to constantly deal with those people. Now I want to be there to help you do that. I love you, Melanie."

"I love you, too."

"That's good to hear." Smiling, Nathan held her arm's length. "Please get Ryan and Andrew. I've got something to ask them."

"I'll get them." A lightness in her step, Melanie hurried back to the waiting area and found Ryan and Andrew busy playing with their Game Boys. "Come on, kids. Nathan wants to talk to you."

Andrew jumped up. "Are you done being mushy?"

"That's enough. Come with me." Melanie heard Juliane's laughter as she went through the swinging doors that led back to the exam rooms.

Melanie hung back as Ryan and Andrew gathered near the bed. Nathan put his hands on their shoulders. "I've got something really important I want to ask you guys. I've been thinking about this for a long time, so I hope you'll say yes. I'd like your permission to marry your mom."

Pressing her lips together, Melanie blinked rapidly to keep the tears at bay as she watched her little boys nod their heads. Andrew held out his hand, and Nathan shook it. Ryan did the same. Then Andrew looked from Nathan to Melanie and back again. "I've been praying every night that you'd marry my mom. So get busy and ask her."

"Come here, Mom. I'd get down on one knee, but it might not be so good in a hospital gown." Nathan extended his hand, and Melanie took it. "Melanie, I love you, and I love Ryan and Andrew. I want us to be a family. Will you marry me?"

"Yes. I love you." Melanie couldn't stop the tears as she embraced the three most important men in her life.

Andrew and Ryan shrugged out of the group hug, and Andrew tapped Nathan on the arm. "You can kiss her now, if you want."

Nathan laughed. "Thanks. I'm going to do that."

"Not too long though."

Melanie closed her eyes and kissed her husband-to-be. When she stepped away, the boys applauded. She looked at Nathan and smiled. "Just right."

* * * * *

Dear Reader,

Thank you for reading *Hometown Dad*, the last of my Kellerville books. I hope you enjoyed Nathan and Melanie's story. Of course, the Ohio setting has a special place in my heart because I met and married my husband there, and our two girls were born while we lived there.

This story is also special for another reason. One of my daughters has Crohn's disease, so I wanted to write a story that would make more people aware of this illness that most often develops between the ages of fifteen and twenty-five. It is a chronic disease with no known cure, but thankfully there are treatments that reduce inflammation and relieve symptoms.

I love to hear from readers. I enjoy your letters and emails so much. You can write to me at P.O. box 16461, Fernandina Beach, Florida 32035, or through my website www.merrillee-whren.com.

May God bless you,

Merrillee Whren

QUESTIONS FOR DISCUSSION

1. At the beginning of the story, Melanie is trying to deal with her unruly boys. Would you have handled the situation any differently? If so, how?

2. Melanie feels overwhelmed as she deals with her finances. Why?

3. During her meeting with Nathan at the bank, what action of his immediately endears him to Melanie? What does this tell you about Nathan?

4. Why does Melanie feel inferior to Nathan? Has there ever been a time when you felt inferior to someone? If so, why?

5. Melanie doesn't have a very good relationship with her deceased husband's parents. Why? Have you ever had to deal with a situation like this? If so, how did you handle it?

6. Nathan's life centers on the bank. Why? What makes him rethink his priorities? Has there been a time when you have had to readjust your priorities?

7. Why is Nathan hesitant to pursue his romantic interest in Melanie? Has there ever been a time when a health issue made you reluctant to participate in an activity? If so, explain.

8. Since her husband's death, Melanie has limited her social life. Why? What circumstance makes her realize she needs to change?

9. Why did Melanie grow up in a string of foster homes? How does this make her feel? Why does she worry that people will find out about her past?

10. As Melanie spends more and more time around the Keller clan, what does she start to want? Why is she afraid she can never have it?

11. When Melanie and Nathan are planning their first real date, what worries her? Do you think it is a legitimate worry? Why?

12. Name the things that concern Melanie about starting a relationship with Nathan. Do you think they are legitimate concerns? Why?

13. What worries Andrew when he finds out about Nathan's Crohn's disease? Why is this a natural thought for this little boy?

14. Despite all the bad things that happened in Melanie's life, she manages to remember that God is with her. How does Romans 8:28 relate to Melanie's situation? Do you see this in your life? Explain.

Love Inspired®

TITLES AVAILABLE NEXT MONTH

Available February 22, 2011

A PLACE TO BELONG
Redemption River
Linda Goodnight

MENDING HER HEART
Judy Baer

A DAD OF HIS OWN
Dreams Come True
Gail Gaymer Martin

A COLORADO MATCH
Deb Kastner

IN A DOCTOR'S ARMS
Lisa Mondello

FAMILY TO THE RESCUE
Moonlight Cove
Lissa Manley

REQUEST YOUR FREE BOOKS!

2 FREE INSPIRATIONAL NOVELS
PLUS 2
FREE
MYSTERY GIFTS

Love Inspired®

YES! Please send me 2 FREE Love Inspired® novels and my 2 FREE mystery gifts (gifts are worth about $10). After receiving them, if I don't wish to receive any more books, I can return the shipping statement marked "cancel." If I don't cancel, I will receive 6 brand-new novels every month and be billed just $4.24 per book in the U.S. or $4.74 per book in Canada. That's a saving of at least 23% off the cover price. It's quite a bargain! Shipping and handling is just 50¢ per book in the U.S. and 75¢ per book in Canada.* I understand that accepting the 2 free books and gifts places me under no obligation to buy anything. I can always return a shipment and cancel at any time. Even if I never buy another book, the two free books and gifts are mine to keep forever.

105/305 IDN FDA5

Name _____ (PLEASE PRINT) _____

Address _____ Apt. # _____

City _____ State/Prov. _____ Zip/Postal Code _____

Signature (if under 18, a parent or guardian must sign)

Mail to the **Reader Service:**
IN U.S.A.: P.O. Box 1867, Buffalo, NY 14240-1867
IN CANADA: P.O. Box 609, Fort Erie, Ontario L2A 5X3

Not valid for current subscribers to Love Inspired books.

**Are you a subscriber to Love Inspired books
and want to receive the larger-print edition?
Call 1-800-873-8635 or visit www.ReaderService.com.**

* Terms and prices subject to change without notice. Prices do not include applicable taxes. Sales tax applicable in N.Y. Canadian residents will be charged applicable taxes. Offer not valid in Quebec. This offer is limited to one order per household. All orders subject to credit approval. Credit or debit balances in a customer's account(s) may be offset by any other outstanding balance owed by or to the customer. Please allow 4 to 6 weeks for delivery. Offer available while quantities last.

Your Privacy—The Reader Service is committed to protecting your privacy. Our Privacy Policy is available online at www.ReaderService.com or upon request from the Reader Service.

We make a portion of our mailing list available to reputable third parties that offer products we believe may interest you. If you prefer that we not exchange your name with third parties, or if you wish to clarify or modify your communication preferences, please visit us at www.ReaderService.com/consumerchoice or write to us at Reader Service Preference Service, P.O. Box 9062, Buffalo, NY 14269. Include your complete name and address.

LIREG11